RYKER
The Mavericks, Book 06

Dale Mayer

RYKER: THE MAVERICKS, BOOK 6
Beverly Dale Mayer
Valley Publishing Ltd.

Copyright © 2019

This is a work of fiction. Names, characters, places, brands, media, and incidents are either the product of the author's imagination or are used fictitiously. Any resemblance to actual events, locales, or persons, living or dead, is entirely coincidental.

ISBN-13: 978-1-773362-88-5
Print Edition

About This Book

What happens when the very men—trained to make the hard decisions—come up against the rules and regulations that hold them back from doing what needs to be done? They either stay and work within the constraints given to them or they walk away. Only now, for a select few, they have another option:

The Mavericks. A covert black ops team that steps up and break all the rules … but gets the job done.

Welcome to a new military romance series by *USA Today* best-selling author Dale Mayer. A series where you meet new friends and just might get to meet old ones too in this raw and compelling look at the men who keep us safe every day from the darkness where they operate—and live—in the shadows … until someone special helps them step into the light.

After his last assignment, Ryker is ready for a rest. And he gets it—but only a few hours …

That's even too long for a geologist kidnapped by guerrillas in the Colombian jungle. Ryker has plenty of experience in jungles around the world but, keeping Manila safe—along with the two men she's traveling with and their injured guide—exposes them for who they are. It quickly becomes apparent, under these most gruelling conditions, which of her party steps up and which plan to step out.

Manila's life has become one of never-ending misery at the hands of her captors as they await word from their bosses, who decide her ultimate fate. That she's hunting platinum doesn't matter to them. Nor that she's fighting against the invasive illegal gold mining taking over parts of the area. When Ryker rescues her from her prison tent, she places her trust in his ability to get her and her team safely away. Not yet realizing she'd be gifting him both her body and her heart too.

Ryker needs to keep them all alive and together long enough to get them out of this hellhole—hopefully alive …

Sign up to be notified of all Dale's releases here!

https://geni.us/DaleNews

Books in This Series

Kerrick, Book 1

Griffin, Book 2

Jax, Book 3

Beau, Book 4

Asher, Book 5

Ryker, Book 6

Miles, Book 7

Nico, Book 8

Keane, Book 9

Lennox, Book 10

Gavin, Book 11

Shane, Book 12

Diesel, Book 13

Jerricho, Book 14

Killian, Book 15

Hatch, Book 16

Corbin, Book 17

Aiden, Book 18

Boxed Sets and Bundles

https://geni.us/Bundlepage

CHAPTER 1

RYKER LANDERS LANDED in California. He'd stayed an extra night in Geneva and had spent it with Mickey and Asher. They'd gone out for dinner, sat down at the lake for a long time, and just generally had a good old time without the pressure and strain of all the action they'd been through. Ryker had no idea where he was going next, but he hoped for a few days off. He headed to his brother's place now. He figured he'd catch a couple days of doing nothing but maybe playing a few video games and something mundane, like mowing the lawn. That sounded good to him. Especially if it came with a cold beer.

He hopped into his vehicle and drove away from the airport. He hated the traffic, the smell and the smog, but something was very comforting about being home again. As he pulled up to his brother's front door, it opened, and his nephew came barreling out. "Ryker, Ryker," he said. "You came."

"I said I would, buddy." He picked him up, tossed him high in the air and laughed.

As he stepped inside, his sister-in-law came over and gave him a kiss. "You look tired."

"Yeah, it's been a bit of a rush," he said. "After a few days here I'll be fine."

His brother, Reggie, walked over, patted his back and

said, "Will they give you a few days?"

"I hope so," he said.

But just over a day later his phone chimed. He looked down and it read, **You ready?**

He thought about it, smiled and answered, **Yes.**

Good, came the reply. **You're heading to the jungle. A geologist has gone missing. Dr. Manila Folgers.**

I could take a whole team in there and still not find him.

And we think *she* has been taken by guerrillas.

The animal variety? he typed, half as a bad joke.

No, the well-armed variety. We need somebody to get her out, without causing a war.

But I like causing wars, Ryker said.

Then cause it with her. She's been looking for platinum, a hot commodity in the world. We're afraid she found some—and someone else found out.

Ouch.

Get ready. You're leaving in the morning.

CHAPTER 2

R YKER STOOD ON the upper deck of the cruiser and studied the coastline. "When he said the Colombian jungle," he muttered to himself, "he meant it." He stared at the heavy overgrowth. Anything one hundred yards from the water was almost a dense thicket, and the best information he could get was that his missing geologist was in the Pacific Region of Colombia. That was the smallest of the five regions and had one major city on the coast that served as a major shipping port. Of course, many small villages were up and down the coast.

He was coming up to Tumaco, the second port in the region, but they were still a long way off the shoreline, and he would have an awful lot of inland traveling to do. Which is why he would travel at night and would get dropped off by a helicopter to Manila's last known location, which had been pulled off the locator on her phone. Then it had gone dead.

Ryker was aiming to land somewhere close to where she'd gone missing last to see if he could track her from there. This was definitely guerrilla territory, and he was not looking forward to being out here without reliable communication while trying to find a woman who was most likely already dead. But apparently not only was she a geologist interested in stopping a lot of the illegal gold mining in the Chocó Department region—good luck with that—but she was also looking for platinum, a resource at a very low ebb around the world, making it even more valuable.

He shook his head. She had come here as part of a group of five, including their two guides to help carry some of the gear and the samples. Normally she went out alone, but, this time, Global Mining Industries had insisted. Her university shared her with Global for these joint pursuits. The team idea was a good thing in theory, but it didn't matter in reality because all of them were missing now. Nobody knew if the guides had been taken prisoner as well or if they had just taken off. As far as Ryker's jaded mind would say though, the guides had been part of the kidnapping too. Gain a few dollars, head back home and nobody would be the wiser. It happened all the time. People went missing in these far corners, and nobody ever came and checked. This was a lawless land here.

Behind him, he heard a slight sound. Being on a navy cruiser, he ignored it.

"Ryker?"

He recognized the voice. Ever so slowly, he turned in surprise. "Miles?"

His old friend reached out a hand, but, rather than shake, they half hugged and smacked each other on the shoulders.

"Damn, it's good to see you," Ryker said. "What the hell are you doing here?"

Miles nodded toward the jungle out there. "Heading back into my worst nightmare," he said with a tilt of his mouth.

It took a moment for Ryker to understand. "Are you coming with me?"

Miles nodded.

"Oh, I remember," Ryker said. "Didn't you get bitten by a viper?"

"Sure did. Lost a chunk of my foot on that deal," Miles said cheerfully.

"So why the hell did you volunteer to come back in?"

"A couple reasons. The primary one being that you need help, and I don't want you in there alone because the odds are against you coming back out again. I don't give a shit what anybody says about this region being a cakewalk. It's not by any stretch of the imagination. Two, I don't want something like that to beat me," he said. "I'd done an awful lot of antiguerrilla warfare training well before we went in the last time, and I had been at the top of my game. Well, until that damn snake bite. I was carried out by my teammates, and I swore—if anybody ever needed me to return again—I'd do it just to help save myself."

"Outside of checking that you were okay, I didn't see much of you after that trip."

"And that trip was a few years ago," Miles admitted. "Don't know about you, but I decided I needed a change of pace."

Ryker snorted. "This is hardly a change of pace."

Miles's British accent came in heavily as he laughed. "But it is," he said. "This is faster and more dangerous but without the brass interference. We can make decisions without having to worry about permission."

"I hear that," Ryker said. "The trouble is, I was always guided—and limited in that way—by my own honor system. And that is always way more intense than whatever the brass deems from above."

"I get you," Miles said, "but still, it's me or nobody."

"Oh, hey. Don't worry. I want you with me," Ryker

said. "I was already trying to figure out how the hell I was supposed to handle this job alone. It's one thing to go in without backup on a small job, but something like this?" He shook his head. "No, I'll be glad to have you at my side."

"Good thing," Miles said, "because it is what it is already."

"Yeah, and it's good," he said. "I wish we had more information though."

"We have the latitude and longitude of the GPS where they were," Miles said. "And I have preliminary files on everybody on the team. But I wonder how we'll get the rest while in the jungle here, blocking any reception. Plus we have nothing on the two guides."

"Gee, what a surprise," Ryker said. "What's the chance they're in on it?"

Miles nodded. "Unfortunately, in Colombia, everybody will take a paycheck or an extra little bit of cash for something like this. The guerrillas keep everybody in the loop. And the guerrillas keep them all on their side by paying them."

"And now the guerrillas are attached to the drug cartels as well, giving the guerrillas access to even more money to buy allegiances," Ryker muttered. "After that one attempt by their government to rehabilitate and to make peace, they've more or less aligned with all the drugs cartels instead."

"And yet, anybody with a brain could have seen that one coming," Miles said. "The authorities got them to surrender and took out half of them, and the rest saw the writing on the wall, then headed back to the jungle. They handed over the bulk of their weapons in this plea or negotiation deal, which was a bad deal for them. A lot of them were put into the land and supposed civilization, but a lot of them couldn't handle it.”

“Isn’t that the truth. Once you’ve been in a war full time, it makes you wonder if you can ever leave it. I’ve had that thought a time or two myself.”

“I know,” Miles said. “I was thinking that this job could be the last one.”

“You too, huh? But then I feel that way about every job,” Ryker said, laughing.

“Right?” Miles said. “I’ve got weapons in our kit all packed up. You should take a look.”

“Good,” he said as he turned to look around at the deck of the cruiser. “Does anybody even know we’re here? I get that everybody knows, but it’s like we don’t exist. It’s a bizarre feeling.”

“Exactly,” Miles said. “And that’s the way they like it. The less they know, the less they have to even think about it. As far as these guys are concerned, we’re here on a secret mission, and that’s it.”

“Well,” Ryker said, “that’s the truth, isn’t it?”

“We’re leaving at midnight, if you’re okay with that.”

“Yeah. We should land just in perfect jaguar-hunting time,” he said with a laugh.

MANILA FOLGERS STAYED huddled in the small tent that she’d been given, and she was damn grateful to have that. Being in the middle of the guerrilla camp was not a good place for a white woman. And particularly not one in her position. She should have known better and *not* listened to her bosses. She’d planned to come all alone—how arrogant and foolish, yes—yet she would’ve been better off alone. As far as she was concerned, one of the guides had given her up and had taken a payout and was even now back in his village, happily laughing at having made a smart move with his guerrilla friends.

She didn't even know which group of guerrillas these were. She thought they were still part of the same FARC group, an acronym for some bloody remnants of an all-powerful guerrilla warfare group back in the nineties and way before. They made a plea deal that had gone bad for a lot of them, and the remainder of the group got more powerful by attaching themselves to a lot of the Colombian drug world.

Not that any of that should have impacted her, but, right now, not only did the guerrillas say that she wasn't allowed to go where she wanted to go, but they also said that she wasn't going anywhere without their permission. She suspected that some of her team might already have been executed too, and that brought on her cold sweats.

The gold mining so rampant in this part of the Colombian countryside was destroying a lot of the natural habitats of this country. It was illegal, and it was destructive, but it was a moneymaker, and everybody was jumping on that bandwagon. She made a mental note anytime she ran across these activities, to share with others more actively working to stop this.

However, she was here solely looking for platinum, something the world was quickly running out of. And there was a good chance some deposits were along here, and she needed to be pulling her samples.

She had all her paperwork in order.

This guerrilla group was so young as a whole. Spoke to the scarcity of jobs in this country. But there were so many of them, and all of them heavily armed. She didn't know what the guerrillas would do with her, and honestly, it sounded like they didn't know what they would do either. She understood Spanish but didn't let them know that. She was deliberately speaking English, but, then again, who knew what her guides had told these guerrillas?

Just then her tent flap flipped back, and a young woman stepped inside. She motioned for Manila to get up. Slowly she got up and stared at her. She motioned again for Manila to walk ahead of her. She walked out of her tent to see her team members also being shepherded over to one side. Both of them thankfully. Just the two guides were missing. She was quite surprised when she and her team were then given water. She quickly washed her face and the back of her neck and then took some to drink.

Her team members looked at her warily.

She shrugged. "No idea," she said quietly. "Just stay cooperative."

"Yes, stay cooperative," said a man from the side, his voice harsh.

She glanced at him as he laughed to see two missing front teeth, but, of course, he carried two rifles, as if that made up for it.

She opened her mouth again and said, "We mean you no harm."

"You're an interfering foreigner. We don't want you here," he snapped.

"If by that you mean, I'm a geologist, and I'm looking for platinum, then, yes."

His face worked as he tried to sort through what that meant.

Somebody on the other side said, "Platinum?"

She turned and nodded. "There's a very good chance

that Colombia has wonderful stores of it. But I won't know until I get some of my samples back to the lab."

"What company do you work for?"

"Global Mining Industries," she said. "I'm sure you've heard of them."

Of course, nothing but blank stares gazed back at her. She lifted the water and took another big drink. It was always a problem to drink enough to compensate for the heat down here. You weren't supposed to drink it all at once. You were supposed to drink it slowly to allow your body to tank back up again. "When can we leave?" she asked.

The man missing two teeth laughed again. "Why should we let you go anywhere?"

"Because I haven't done you any harm," she said quietly. "We're here with your government's permission."

"We don't give a shit about our government," Toothless said. "If you don't pay the price for being here with us, then we don't have to let you do anything."

"Ah," she said with a nod. "So this is just about money."

"It's not just about money," he said, getting angry. Then a shout came from across the path. It was almost a road, but there were no vehicles. They were all on foot. Immediately Toothless subsided. He shouldered his rifle and turned and walked away.

She glanced at her team members. "Hold on," she said.

"We should never have come," Andy announced.

"Nope, you shouldn't have," the second guerrilla said. "It makes no sense that you're here, unless you're spies."

She stared at him in surprise. "Of course we're not spies. We didn't even know you were here."

He didn't like that answer either. Whether his ego thought that everybody should know where they were or whether he had some other reason for that, she didn't know. But his glare told her that he definitely didn't like her answer. She shrugged and waited for whatever would happen next. She didn't have to wait long. Two other gunmen joined them, and these were immediately visible as the bosses.

She smiled and held out a hand. "Thank you very much," she said. "The water is much welcome."

One stared down at her hand and said, "Why are you here?"

She quickly repeated how she sought platinum here.

"Seriously?"

"It's a valuable mineral, and it's needed in the world."

"Potentially," he said. "You sure you aren't after the gold?"

She shook her head. "The illegal gold mining in this area is vast. What's that got to do with me searching for platinum?"

"Maybe nothing," he said, "but we have to at least check it out."

"Feel free to do that. I just don't know how you would."

"We're not so cut off from the world as you may think," he said. "I already have men on it."

"Good," she said. She went to lift her backpack off her back, when immediately several rifles were pointed at her. She froze. She lifted her head to stare at the leader. "I can show you some rocks of what I'm looking for and want to ask if you had seen anything like it."

He motioned at her to continue.

Slowly she opened the flap to her backpack, wondering how this bag had even been left with her in the first place. Their other bags had been taken, but this one she had been given back to keep—which held her laptop and her samples. Her personal belongings were long gone though, she figured. She pulled out several rocks, looking for the one she wanted. When she found it, she held it up.

"I'm looking for rocks like this," she said, "that contain platinum. This is what we're looking for," she repeated. "Have you seen more of these rocks?"

He studied the rock and then shrugged. "It looks much like the other rocks of our region."

"Yes, and no," she said. "Look at these colors here and look at the markings." With a disinterested shake of his head, she pulled out some of her maps and some of the satellite photos she had. Then she spread out the map and awkwardly placed on it several of the images that she had, as of course there was no table and nobody stepped forward to help her. "We're looking for outcroppings like this. There's a lot more to it than that, but that would give us a general direction."

"And why should we help you?"

She just blinked at him. "Well, I suppose it would get us out of your hair much faster."

"I don't have to worry about that," he said. "Nobody is coming after you."

"Why is that?"

"Because they'll try to deal with our government, but our government doesn't deal with us," he said with a flat stare. "We're in a cold war at the moment with them."

"Ah, I understand," she said and then proceeded to act as if she had no clue what he just said. "So have you seen any of these outcroppings?" She glanced around at the rocks around them, then pointed. "It'd be like that but bigger and longer. We're looking for different color tones here." She pointed at the side of her rock sample, and he shook his head.

"No, I don't think so."

But from the other side of her came a spat of Spanish.

Manila understood most of it, but it was a different dialect than what she was accustomed to. Somebody thought that they had seen something. She glanced at one woman. "So, was that a yes that you have seen this?" she asked hopefully.

A young woman stepped forward. She had on a camouflage T-shirt that hung down past her pants pockets and was dressed like many of the soldiers. She pointed off to the right. And then she talked to the leader in another spat of rapid-fire Spanish so thick with her accent that it was almost impossible to pick up.

But the Spanish itself was fairly clear. This girl had seen something. A large series of rocks were a couple miles from here. The leader asked her if the rocks looked like this, and she nodded.

"Any chance I can see it?"

"Why would we let you do that?"

"Well, the platinum is very valuable," she said. "And, in the right hands, it would offer an awful lot of power and negotiation for your region."

He stared at her for a long moment.

"And, of course, none of that makes any difference," she said, "if I can't actually see it and if we can't take some samples back."

He frowned at that.

And she could see that he was desperately trying to find the right response, but, at the same time, he didn't really want anything to do with her and her plans. "I can probably tell when I see it," she said. "I can't tell if it's platinum for sure until I see it and test it."

He frowned at her again for that and then shrugged. "Maybe," he said. Then he turned and walked away. As he turned, he called and ordered to have them all taken back to a tent.

She quickly had another sip of water and then tried to take the water with her, but it was removed from her hand. Expecting that, she didn't say anything more, but they were all put into one tent, which was interesting. The rest of her team asked, "Are you okay?"

"Of course I am," she said. "Now it's a case of whether we'll get a chance to see that rock formation or not."

"Are you expecting them to take you?" Andy asked, surprised.

"Expecting, no, but considering it could be valuable, it's in their best interests. Besides, we have to do what we can to stay alive," she said. "They don't believe anybody will come to our rescue, but I do."

"And why would anybody?" asked her other team member. Andy was the young kid on the block, but Benjamin was the older, grumpier one and very pessimistic. "It's not as if the company gives a shit."

"Well, considering I already told Global that I found one vein of platinum that looked very possible," she said calmly, "I highly doubt that."

"Well, the chances are they had your GPS at the same time that they lost track of us," Benjamin said. "All they'll do is keep that for future reference. Not to save us now. Maybe to send in another team with more weapons."

"*More* weapons?"

"Sure," he said. "I had a handgun with me, and they took it."

"I did too," Andy said.

She nodded. "Of course. Enough predators are out here of the four-legged variety to justify any number of weapons. But, to kill the guerrillas, that won't be wise."

"We didn't realize they were in this area," Andy said. "We did as much research as we could, but we certainly weren't planning to do them any harm."

"No, but you came to Colombia," Benjamin said. "You might as well be prepared to come up against guerrillas."

"How far off the coast are we, do you think?" Manila asked everyone.

"Maybe twenty miles, twenty-five miles," Andy said. "Why?"

She shrugged. "That'll be our easiest way out of here."

He snorted. "No way. That's not just twenty-something miles but that's miles of the Colombian jungle. More snakes and venomous animals are in this part of the world than anywhere."

"Sure," she said, "but we have a scheduled pickup in just four days."

"Do you think that will happen?"

"We were supposed to return the other direction," she said, "to make our rendezvous. I highly doubt we'll get there."

"So what good will the coast do?"

"It'll only do us any good if we can get some help there," she said, "but it's at least a decent option to try."

"Well, that won't happen," Benjamin said. "You know, no one is coming."

"They will," she said. "For that reason alone, we need to make sure that we help the guerrillas in whatever way they think is necessary."

"And that won't end well either," Benjamin said. "Have you forgotten who is the white woman here?"

She stiffened at that. "I've forgotten nothing," she said. "I might be worth getting a ransom paid."

"True," Andy said with a smile. "Have you told the guerrillas that?"

"No, not yet," she said. "But they're not stupid. They're dealing with the drug cartels in this part of the world, so those might be the groups who are more interested in keeping me, just because I'm worth money."

"Keeping *you* alive," Benjamin said with a snort. "Who gives a shit about the rest of us, right?"

"I'm not even getting into that discussion with you," she said in an exhausted voice. "Did anybody consider the fact that maybe the guides were in on this?"

Silence came from the other two.

She nodded. "I was thinking the older man was part of it. It sucks, but it makes sense."

"Well, it makes sense that everybody here is corrupt," Andy said. "But you're right. He's the one who seemed to be always a little bit off to the side, as if waiting to be taken out."

"Right," she said, "and I don't know what happened to the younger one."

"Who knows?" Benjamin said, flopping flat on his back. "I wonder how long they plan on keeping us here."

"Until they figure out what to do with us is my guess," she said quietly. "I don't know how long that'll be, but I highly doubt it'll be anytime soon."

Benjamin stared up at the tent roof and said, "And will they feed us, or will they have us suffer a little bit?"

"You could always try to stay positive," she said gently.

He shook his head. "I'm a realist. You can be the funny optimist."

She snorted. "I'm a geologist. We find a needle in a haystack, and you can go an entire lifetime without finding anything."

"But you did find something, didn't you?" Andy asked eagerly.

She smiled at him. "Yes, I think I did. But I know more is around here. If I could get to wherever that rock outcropping is that the woman talked about, that would be huge." She pulled out her maps and laid them on the ground, then studied them. "So, based on where we're at here"—she took a pencil and put a small *X*—"that's the next-best location. And, if we can't get there, Global has a location to check out in the future."

Andy leaned over and nodded. They pulled out their satellite images, and he said, "I think that's the peak up on the back side of the tent here."

She studied that, nodded and circled it lightly. "So, based on that, and where the woman was standing ..." She immediately lined herself up, looking at the photo, and then put a pointer in the direction the woman had indicated.

Andy turned the photo ever-so-slightly to line up and said, "So she's talking about anywhere in this direction. A couple miles or something, I think."

"Yes," she said, "so that's possible."

"Maybe," he nodded, "but it doesn't exactly match up to the terrain we were looking for."

"And that's the problem with platinum," she said. "Actually it's the problem with any rocks. You'd think you're in the best-guess location for its natural geography, but it doesn't always work out that way. Sometimes we find something that makes no sense. Most of the time it works the way we think it does, but then there's that one odd time where it'll be something that you didn't recognize, and it'll be more underground than aboveground."

He nodded. "But still, what's the answer?"

She laughed. "The answer is easy. We need to return to the field."

CHAPTER 3

MANILA MEANT IT when she said that they needed to return, but it wouldn't happen this trip. She also meant it when she said somebody would surely come. She wanted to finish her job here, but that was looking impossible now. She turned to look back at the two men. "How many guerrillas do you think were out there?"

She deliberately kept her voice low. She didn't want anybody else listening in if possible, but chances were that somebody was parked right outside their tent. She could see long-enough shadows along three sides that confirmed nobody was terribly close, but she couldn't tell if someone was sitting out front. Then again, the guerrillas were also probably confident that nobody could escape. Everyone knew how dangerous this area was. Her two team members looked at each other and frowned.

"Eight?" Andy said, his voice equally soft.

She looked at Benjamin. "You?"

He held up his hand as he started counting the ones he could remember. Then he shrugged and said, "Eight or nine." He looked around. "Doesn't mean another couple dozen aren't close by though."

"I know," she said. "I'm wondering if this is an offshoot or like a warning party or if this is just one of the groups checking out the lay of the land or if somebody specifically told them that we were here, so they came with a small party to take us."

"Anybody's guess," Benjamin said as he stretched out on the ground. "What I do know is, if they plan to march us through the jungle, we need rest."

She thought about it and nodded. "I agree. Easier said than done though. We also haven't eaten much."

"No," Andy said, "and I could use food."

"You probably won't get anything for quite a while," Benjamin said. "So you might as well just give up on that concept."

Andy looked at her, and she shrugged and said, "I don't know about that, but, if they want us alive, they'll feed us. And, if they want us dead, why would they have kept us alive so far?"

"Because they've gone back to their bosses to figure out what to do?" Andy guessed.

She nodded. "I agree. Which means we should be okay until at least tomorrow," she said cheerfully. She shuffled to the edge of the tent beside her maps. "You guys sleep. I'll study these a bit."

Benjamin snorted. "Yeah, well, you do that. Waste of time though."

Andy laid down beside her. "Do you really think we'll find anything here?"

"It's not that easy to tell," she said, thoughtfully tapping the map. "Obviously, if the guerrillas would give us free rein to walk around, it would be a whole lot easier to do our job. But, if they won't let us, then hopefully they'll let us go, and we can return to Global, and they can deal with it themselves."

"And deal how though?" Andy asked. "Send out a bigger

party?"

She shrugged. "Honestly, there isn't an easy answer. If this whole area is swarming with guerrillas who don't want us on the land, then that's a problem. If they wanted something that Global can give them to grant us free passage through here, that's a different story. But mining in a state like this will be a problem too."

"Did you mean that about all the gold mines?" Andy asked.

"You know about that," she said. "The gold mining here is incredibly criminal. But it still only accounts for less than one point five percent of the gold pulled out of the world. So a lot of people want to keep the gold mining to themselves. I'm not looking for gold, and that could be part of the issue here. They might not believe me."

"And, if you are looking for gold, why do they care?"

"Some people are in favor of mining, particularly if they're getting the money. Those against it are losing something. Either losing out on the money, land, freedom and so on. I'm not for any of it because the illegal mining activity is done in such a way that it's damaging the ground around it, and more care could be taken with the byproducts," she said calmly. "That's the part that I deal with, but you can bet nobody's listening to me."

"Because too much money is being made, right?" Andy said.

She smiled. As a university student, he was a brainiac but lacking any real-world experience. This was his first trip out, although he had done a couple trips into the northern BC area for uranium. Then she had too, but looking for platinum was a whole different story. And it wasn't an easy mineral to find.

Some people always wanted to stop you from doing what you wanted to do, and always a lot of people wanted to make sure they got in on whatever it was you were doing. Commerce was the backbone of any society. She just wished that she was anywhere but here right now. And really she wished that she had a chance to check out the rock cropping that the woman had mentioned.

Manila had been here for days with no luck finding anything. It wasn't all that unusual, but, given their starting position, they thought that this area would hold pretty decent odds of finding platinum. And they had lots of rock samples, but nothing that looked terribly promising—except for the one site. Still, she wasn't expecting that site to be a motherlode but more an indication that this area held promise.

She had planned to be here for ten days, and they'd spent six so far. But, with the tour guides gone and them now prisoners of the guerrillas, she knew that her geological trip would get cut short. Yet her stay in Colombia may be extended.

She hoped her faith in Global wasn't misplaced and that someone was coming to rescue them. The last thing she wanted was for her aging mother to have to deal with this loss too. The loss of her father not too long ago and her sister when she was much younger had left just the two of them now. This wasn't the way Manila wanted to go out. She wanted to see so much more of the world, and she wanted to do so much more. She sent out a silent cry in the night. *If somebody's out there and listening, please come help.*

THE NIGHT DROP had been successful, a textbook drop as far as Ryker was concerned, a landing though, that had been a bit of a bitch. No clear landing spot was always a problem, so, with only a thin strip of relatively open space available, yet surrounded by thick forests of trees, he knew it would be touch-and-go. He'd done his best, but, of course, his chute had hung up high above him. He quickly cut his ties and his harness and then slowly lowered himself to the ground. His comm connected him to Miles, and Ryker had already heard his friend fluently swearing as he came down in the trees too.

Ryker muffled his laughter and whispered, "I'm down."

"Well, I will be too. Give me a moment," Miles snapped. "I'm about twelve feet off the ground though."

"Sounds about normal," Ryker said. He checked out the area, but it was silent. "I'm registering you about 242 yards to my left."

"Stay there," Miles said. "You're closer to our target. I'll meet you."

While he waited for Miles to show up, Ryker quickly checked his compass and his GPS. They were off by about half a mile. Not bad for a nighttime landing in these conditions. Of course, this was only the last place that they had this woman's data. She and her team could be anywhere by now. Whether the team was lost or had been caught by guerrillas was hard to say, but a satellite feed had shown them marching through the jungle, and they were not alone. Further investigation had shown that they weren't heading back to any of the main research camps they'd planned to be at.

Still, Ryker was here now, and time was of the essence. Not only was the gold-mining big business here but, between the gold and the drugs, nobody really wanted any intruders, whether scientists or not. And, if she wasn't prepared to pay her way out, then chances were she wouldn't get out at all.

She'd traveled with a team of five, which included two guides. So, two company personnel and the two local guides. He suspected that the guides were long gone. That left her and the other two members of her team. Ryker had read up on them.

One was Benjamin, with over a decade of time with the company. Previously he had been a prospector without a degree behind him but decades of hands-on experience. He didn't put much stock in new technology and held more of a grumpy old-timer attitude than anything.

Manila had a young university student carrying the rock samples. They always needed somebody for the grunt work, and, as long as they could get in and get out, time and time again, it was fine. But she was down for a ten-day excursion, and then she was supposed to return to Bogotá and head to another location—all of this by helicopter or plane, depending on how far away she was going, when she wasn't on foot.

This trip had been planned as far out as one year earlier, but then was tweaked, finalized and booked six weeks ago, checking out what looked like to be the best spots for platinum that Manila had located in previous on-site searches. Still, this ongoing project came down every year to what looked like the best locations each time. They took various samples, went back, analyzed them and then set up the trip for the next time.

She now had three days left on a ten-day trip here. Day seven had started. She'd been taken early on day six. So they were about twenty-four hours into captivity. Those hours could mean a lifetime, depending on how they were treated. Ryker could only hope that the guerrillas saw some value in her and her samples, at least for a ransom demand. But Ryker wasn't sure anybody here could be bothered with that.

It was much easier to shoot intruders dead and leave them for the wild animals, then move on to a different area. When the guerrillas returned in a few months, nothing would be left of their victims except for a few bones scattered around, but that would be it. The jungle was very good at cleaning up their dead.

Miles approached on the left. Ryker didn't even bother looking up.

"I could have been a jaguar, you know," Miles half-joked with that low voice of his. Something about that British accent carried so well.

"Nah, a jaguar would have been a lot quieter," Ryker teased. He looked up with a grin to see Miles's sneer. "We're about a half mile out," Ryker said. "Let's go." They lifted their packs, and he readjusted the weight of his, then his buckles, tightening them before starting off. The heat and humidity were pretty overwhelming, and yet, it was still nighttime.

The trouble with being in this area was he needed to be fully clothed, the heat be damned, not daring to take a chance with short sleeves or bare legs because of the creeping predators around. Some of the damn mosquitoes would take painful chunks from your skin, leaving a maddening itch behind, and that didn't even consider the viruses and diseases they carried and could be transmitted with each bite.

And then there were the venomous vipers and the downright deadly scorpions.

Moving at a steady pace, Ryker and Miles headed toward their last known location for the woman and her team. It didn't take Ryker and Miles long after studying the location from the shadow of the trees. It was an opening wide enough for a dozen tents to have gone up and looked like it might have been an old mining camp used for decades.

Miles whispered behind him, "What do you think? That they set up camp here, despite being one of the well-traveled places?"

"From their point of view, it makes sense, doesn't it?"

"Unfortunately," Miles nodded. "But that would have just brought in anybody else traveling this trail."

"They probably were told, but they weren't trying to hide," he said. "I highly suspect the guides were keeping them out in the open to make them easy to find."

"Sure, but that's you," Miles said. "You always look on the negative side."

"No, I always look for the betrayal from within," Ryker said. "And, more often than not, I'm right."

"Sucks, doesn't it?" Miles said as he motioned to a series of broken leaves. "Nobody even made any attempt to hide their trail."

"That's because the guerrillas think they and their related brotherhood are all alone out here. Not only do they consider this their backyard but they also consider it their playground. And nobody ever suspects another supposed team member when intruding into their space."

"Too damn bad," Miles said, "because, like you said, too often the betrayal is from within."

After taking photographs of the area where the team was last seen, Ryker and Miles quickly held to the trail, obviously leading them away from that spot. When Ryker caught sounds of voices up ahead, they froze and melted into the background to one side. In his comm, Ryker could hear Miles tapping away, giving him a head count of possible hostiles. Ryker crouched down and studied the small group in front of him. Eight people, maybe nine by his count, which was confirmed by Miles' tally too. So where were the sentries? There should be at least two of those out here.

It was a mixed group, including a young woman and a young man, but then the guerrillas were all about gaining new members and improving their numbers. It was a perfect alliance of young and old. Ryker wondered what the actual life expectancy was for any of them. For the women, in particular, chances were they ended up pregnant, bringing children into a world that had very little in the way of modern medicine. He didn't know the stats but couldn't imagine that the life expectancy of a baby born in this scenario was very good either.

As he studied the two young people, they kissed and disappeared into a tent. Just what Ryker expected. Free love reigned everywhere here.

As he watched four of the men laughing and joking, he realized just how short on female members they were. But that wasn't his problem. One tent was off to the side that everybody seemed to be facing but ignoring. Ryker tapped back the location to Miles and got an almost instant response.

I'll check it out.

Ryker waited and watched to see if anybody would notice when Miles slipped around to the side. But he was as good as Ryker was. Miles moved from tree to tree, his shadow blending in and moving with the light. As others moved, so did he. Any sounds he made were covered up by the others' movements. It was quite efficient and elegant. Ryker watched his buddy and waited.

Several of the men got up and headed into the other

tents themselves, but two men were left outside. They were on duty, so Ryker assumed those were the sentries. The interesting thing though was that they didn't care about the space around them. But then they were young, and they weren't well trained, and they were also overconfident about their backyard. Big mistake.

Well, what they didn't understand was that now two human scorpions they weren't expecting would take off with their guests.

The sentries stood and walked together out of the camp in a northerly direction.

There was activity in one tent. Ryker knew perfectly well that was where the couple had gone. Meanwhile, from the other corner, there was nothing but one silent tent. The two sentries walked maybe fifty feet away, then stopped and took a look around before coming back to the camp. They headed down the path, passing him in the night. Then they went for another fifty-odd feet and turned around and returned to camp and sat again.

Ryker's eyebrows rose at that. Very untrained. That wouldn't count for a perimeter check at all in his book.

Miles was already at the back of the silent tent now. The question was, how to check to see who was inside. The opening was in the front, and that would make life a little bit difficult, even with these two lazy sentries. Plus these tents were cheap army-issued units, so not much in the way of ventilation windows. Still, a sharp knife would take care of the canvas in no time.

Just as he wondered how Miles was getting on, a double tap came on his comm. He tapped back once. And then came three more. His eyebrows shot up. In a hoarse whisper, he asked, "All three?" Back came the affirmative *Yes*. Ryker booked it. He snuck down and around, so he wasn't crossing the path right in front of these two supposed guards and came up behind Miles from a distance. Ryker kept his eye on the sentries in the front of the captives' tent, but they were talking carelessly. And then they got up and did their pass to the far side again.

As Ryker watched, they passed him again and went down the other path. They should have been breaking apart and individually going in a big circle around this camp, but that wasn't what they were up to. As they reentered the camp, he was already at Miles's side.

He peered inside to see three white people sleeping. Two males and one female. Not dressed the same as the other guerrillas and one with a backpack and what looked like maps, so these were the three he had come for.

Good. That was nice and easy. Now all he had to do was get their cooperation and then get them out of here. But that would take a little bit longer. He quickly gave Miles the relay times on the sentries and their system of patrol, or lack of one.

Miles nodded and, working as quietly as he could, finished slicing open the back of the tent. All three of them inside slept without noticing anything. But then the heat would do that to them too. Not to mention the fact that, if they hadn't had much in the way of food, they would be weak and tired.

Just then, the sentries rose and headed out of the camp toward the north again. At that, both Miles and Ryker snaked a hand around each of the male captives' mouths. Both men woke up, fighting to get a breath, but, as soon as Ryker and Miles explained who they were, both men subsided. Then Ryker went toward Manila. Her eyes opened even before he could get close to her. She opened her mouth, and he held up a finger and said, "*Shh.*"

SHE IMMEDIATELY SNAPPED her mouth closed and studied his features. He was white-skinned, and, in the dark, even that would be obvious. She turned to the other two men of her team, both of them sneaking out the new back flap of the tent. She raced to her maps and quickly packed everything up, even as the stranger waited impatiently. She just glared at him but stayed quiet. Then she took her backpack, and he shook his head and took it from her and then pushed her to go outside the tent. But she wanted the backpack.

He glared at her and pointed.

She hissed, "Make sure it comes," and stepped from the tent. Up ahead, her two team members were led farther away from the tent. She quickly followed, being as quiet as possible, but it wasn't easy. She was tired, and it was dark.

He stayed behind her, knowing that at any moment, they could get separated. He waited and watched as the sentries came back and passed through the tent section, then carried on down south. He raced behind the others.

As soon as she turned and saw him, her gaze went right to her backpack. She nodded and kept on going.

RYKER DIDN'T GIVE her a chance to stop, and he could see Miles leading the men quickly away. Ryker didn't know how far they had traipsed, but they were leaving a trail a mile wide. Couldn't be helped when there were five of them, and three didn't know how to slide secretly through the jungle. He took some time every once in a while to clean up as they went. It wouldn't fool any real tracker, but maybe it could fool these kids.

Ryker kept on going until he noticed the woman stayed with him. He studied her closely in the half-light. She wasn't panicked nor appeared to be anxious in any way. "Why aren't you with the others?"

"Because you're slowing down, trying to hide our path," she said. "And I won't leave you alone." She almost sighed when she said the last part, and he rolled his eyes at her. "So *hurry*." She glared at him, but she turned and immediately moved faster.

He raced up behind her, grabbed her hand to keep her with him as they ran and whispered, "We have to catch up."

She nodded and started running. Of course, it sounded like a herd of elephants going through the brush, and that would immediately cause them more problems. He bent down and scooped her into his arms.

She gasped in outrage.

"I have to do it this way to keep you quiet." He glared at her.

With a sniff, she subsided. "How is it you can run so quietly?"

"Practice," he said. Between her and her backpack and his own bags, he knew he could manage a couple miles but not too much more. But the more miles they put between them and the gang of teenage guerrillas behind them, the better. If they were ever caught again, the guerrillas would not be so easy on any of them.

He kept running until they could see the others up ahead. At the sound of his footsteps, Miles immediately moved the others off the path. Ryker smiled at that and let out an odd whistle. It sounded like an owl, a cry of a bird of prey. Immediately Miles responded with an answering cry.

Ryker slowed when he caught up with them and lowered her to the ground. One of the other men, the tall young kid, stepped forward and asked her, "Are you okay?"

She wrinkled her face up at him. "I'm okay," she said. "But apparently I was making too much noise."

The kid looked at her in surprise and looked up at the man behind her. "Thank you for the rescue," he said, his voice heartfelt. "I'm Andy." He pointed at the other man and said, "He's Benjamin, and Manila is our geologist."

Ryker nodded. "I'm Ryker. He's Miles. Let's go." And that was all he would say, but he moved them rapidly, his hands pushing and shoving to give them an idea of just how fast they had to move. And, with Miles leading, they headed off again. As soon as she made more noise, she winced and looked at him, and he nodded. "One more like that," he said, "and you'll get carried."

She glared at him, and he grinned. But he knew his teeth were flashing white in all this jungle darkness, and that would get a bullet between his jaws if he didn't watch it.

It didn't take long to come across more guerrillas. These were an older bunch, fully armed and more experienced. Ryker could imagine what they had gone through to live to be this old in their line of work. Miles and Ryker tapped out their strategy; then Miles took Manila's two team members first, detouring deeper into the brush. Waiting a good thirty minutes, then Ryker carried Manila to meet up with the others. Another couple hours later, they heard more voices.

Following us? Ryker tapped out to Miles.

It took a minute or so before Miles responded. **Can't**

see them. Heard two on patrol. So I think not.

Finally, after four hours total on the run since being rescued, Manila stumbled to a stop, gasping. Her two team members were almost done too. Ryker looked at Miles and nodded. "We need a place for them to rest."

"I think I hear water," Miles said.

"And that brings its own dangers," Ryker warned.

Miles nodded. "We need to go up farther toward a pool off the river."

"Just make sure you pick one that's not jaguar-infested," Ryker said.

So the two softly wrangled back and forth.

Ryker quickly picked out a stand of trees, and, boosting Manila to the lower of the branches, he came up behind her. When they got up about another ten feet, he removed several other branches too, hacking at them with a machete, and made a crossways platform that would hide them from people below. There he pointed out a very large branch and said, "You can rest up there."

Nodding obediently, she sank against the trunk and, with her eyes closed, took several deep breaths.

"If you think you can sleep here, I have ropes to tie you to the limb, if you want that added security."

She nodded. "Maybe later."

Ryker pulled water from his backpack and handed it to her.

She looked at it in surprise and then drank greedily. Then she stopped suddenly and looked at him with a guilty expression.

He shook his head. "Yes, you shouldn't drink too much at a time, but drink up whatever's left," he said. "We'll refill it as soon as we get fresh water."

She nodded and quickly emptied the bottle. When she handed it back to him, he slung both his backpacks up on a higher branch and pulled out a canteen and another bottle.

"I'll be back," Ryker told her. "Don't move, and don't make a sound."

And, with that, he scampered down the tree.

CHAPTER 4

M ANILA STARED AFTER him, but he completely disappeared within seconds. She'd never seen anybody move so quietly or so rapidly in these kinds of conditions. She was exhausted, and she'd sweated so much that her body was almost completely dehydrated already. She needed that water so badly, but she also needed rest. She stretched out, chest down, and laid her head on the huge tree branch and closed her eyes.

But knowing that he was getting water and would be coming back up again stopped her from dropping into a deep sleep—that and possibly falling off her perch should she roll over, forgetting where she was. She needed to find out who he was and where they were going. The fact of the matter was, they were heading in the same direction where the woman had mentioned the rock cropping was, and Manila knew that she'd get nothing but an absolute stink for even considering it, but she was desperate to see if that was the rock formation she sought. And she also knew that the chances of making that happen were zero to none. She'd try to make her case if she could catch her breath again though.

Hearing a sudden noise below her, and knowing that the trees were home to predators of all kinds, she froze. She looked around and up, but nothing was above her. And, just as suddenly, causing her heart to freeze and a gasp of shock to escape, Ryker's face popped through the fronds. He handed her a water bottle and said, "Here. This one's for you. Don't guzzle this one. Just take a sip as you need it."

She nodded and whispered, "Thank you."

And that white, toothy smile of his flashed again.

"I'm Manila," she said.

"Ryker."

She thought that had been his name, but it was unusual enough that she wanted to hear it again. But then hers was unusual too. She groaned as she carefully rolled onto her back, glad to see that the limb was where she had imagined it under the additional fronds atop it. "I'm so sore," she whispered, her eyes closed again.

"And you will be for a few days," he said. "We won't get out of this fast or easy."

"Who sent you?" she murmured.

"American government."

At that, her gaze popped open, and she stared at him in wonder. "Seriously?"

He shrugged. "Black ops. So nobody in the government will acknowledge that I'm here."

She almost laughed at that. "I presume Global, my company, contacted you guys?"

"I'm not sure," he said. "I got my orders that you were here and to come and get you."

"But how did you know I was specifically here?" she asked.

"GPS reading on your last recorded phone call," he said.

She stared up in the sky and whispered, "Thank heavens. I tried and tried for hours to get a call through, and everybody kept telling me not to worry about it since I couldn't get any connection. But I climbed a tree and managed to get through."

"Well, that final attempt saved your life."

"What will the guerrillas do when they find out we're gone?"

"Tell their bosses, get into a lot of shit, and we could end up with five times that many gunmen after us," he said. "And every one of them will be well-armed."

"I noticed how young they were," she said.

"I know," he said. "Almost too young." But he didn't elaborate.

She didn't need him to. That woman probably wasn't even sixteen, but the soldier she was with had his hands all over her. "It's not much of a life for them, is it?"

"It's all they really know. Plus they have a huge built-in family instantly," he said. "They belong to something, to someone, and that makes a big difference in their lives."

"I don't see how it could," she said. "There's no education, arts or normal family life."

"Nothing is normal about any of it. And our life isn't normal to a lot of people in many places of the world," he said. "Stop talking and rest."

She almost laughed at that. "Are you always so short on words?"

"You're wearing yourself out. You need to conserve your energy, and we need to be quiet."

At that, he closed his eyes, and she could watch everything unplug as his body reset. She didn't know how he did it, and she wasn't sure if she'd follow suit, but she switched, gently rolling over again, so she was draped over this huge branch. Then she closed her eyes and slept.

When she woke again, Ryker stared at her. She focused on him, blurry-eyed. "How is it you look bright-eyed and bushy-tailed?"

"It's not a term I understand, but, if you mean alert, it's because of my training."

She dropped her head back down onto the hard branch and groaned. "I'm used to rough conditions," she said, slowing turning over, her back to the tree limb now. "And I'm used to hiking all over hell and beyond looking for rocks. I'm a geologist after all, but I can't say I've ever slept in a tree before."

"If you're lucky," he said cheerfully, "this will be the last time on this trip. But, other than that, you could find that we'll be in one every day."

"Don't leopards go up trees?"

"I'm sure they do," he said. "Not to mention the guerrilla sentries have their favorite lookouts. So up on the top is much better. But then, when you're too high up, you'll be looking down, and there'll be no way to see what's going on underneath."

"What about the snakes?" she asked.

He looked at her curiously. "I didn't figure geologists would be worried about snakes."

"Well, I don't generally go where there's very many, and I'm always wearing boots," she said. "But the snakes here— the anacondas and the boas—the ones that hang off the trees and just snatch you up, … they're bigger than life."

"And yet, you came here?"

She nodded. "I did. I'm looking for platinum, and that is the problem. I agreed to do these searches, but Global was also supposed to keep us safe."

"And yet, you wanted to come without a team, I understand?"

She winced at that. "I was thinking that maybe it would

be easier if I came alone or just with somebody to carry my gear. I didn't really want two guides with us."

"And how do you feel now?"

"Honestly, I think the guides had something to do with us being captured." At his stare of surprise, she nodded. "The old guy was too suspicious. He was always standing off to one side, as if waiting for something to happen. I don't know about the young one, but it's possible that the older one betrayed him as well. Neither of them are here, so I rather imagine the guerrillas either told them to take a hike and paid them off or said that they would get paid down the road. I don't know." She shrugged. "The bottom line is, they were freed because they're locals, and we weren't."

Just then she heard a weird sound. "What's that?"

He held up a finger, tilted his head and pushed something against his ear. She realized he was in communication with his partner. "Someone's coming," he whispered. "Not a sound."

She stared up at him in horror, and she remembered how dark it had been, and yet, how much of a trail they'd probably left behind. She winced. If she'd brought this on them, she'd be incredibly sorry. But she couldn't do anything about it now except follow instructions and stay as quiet as possible.

Ryker didn't even breathe as his gaze bored into hers. Only his attention wasn't on her. He was listening to everything around them. She couldn't hear anything, but she assumed he heard everything with how intense his gaze was. The problem was, just what did he hear?

RYKER HEARD THE footsteps underneath them, but they weren't as he expected. It wasn't the steady footfall of somebody either tracking them or a group following somebody else's lead. It was more of a limping and broken walk. He frowned at that and peered through the surrounding brush to get his suspicions confirmed. He grabbed a few of the details and then whispered to her, leaning over so he was above her. "The younger guide, did he have on a blue-and-white shirt with a tattoo on the side of his neck?"

She frowned and then quickly nodded.

"He's below, but he's dragging a leg. Was he injured before?"

She quickly shook her head and then placed her mouth near his ear, heat swiftly moving between them as she whispered, "We have to help him. Pablo is a young man, his whole life ahead of him."

Ryker shook his head in an instant. "He could be a diversion." She stared at him in horror, and he nodded, then continued, "They'll drag us out of hiding with an injured friend."

"Doesn't mean he isn't injured," she said. "They might have tortured him."

He nodded. "Possible, but we're not moving."

She took a long shuddering breath and closed her eyes, waiting.

He stayed where he was above her, letting his weight rest gently on top of her to keep her where she was. There was no way to avoid the softness of her breasts beneath him or her pelvic bones positioned perfectly in place to where he was. He swore under his breath, realizing that he couldn't have picked a worse position. But it was what it was.

Ten minutes later, after the sounds of the shuffling of

the injured man headed toward the water, Ryker heard two more sets of footsteps and, this time, rapid ones. He placed a finger against Manila's lips to keep her quiet.

She stared up at him in shock, and he nodded. "That's them coming to check on him."

She let out a slow breath again and whispered, "Bastards."

He reached down, kissed her cheek gently, and said, "It's a continual war to them. And you need to be aware that they might kill him too."

At that, her horrified gaze filled with tears.

He dropped his forehead against hers and whispered, "We can't do anything about it right now."

She turned mute and pursed her lips for a good minute before she finally whispered, "You could."

"It depends if it's already over with or not," he said with a frown.

"You could leave me."

He gave her a look and whispered, "Not happening."

Finally, several other footsteps headed in the opposite direction, laughing and joking. She glared at him with tears in her eyes, and he nodded. "But we don't know anything for sure yet," he said. He waited a good ten minutes before tapping his comm and sending a message.

Miles immediately responded. **Injured man's by the water. But he's bleeding heavily.**

Savable?

Hard to say. The predators will find him soon.

He's young. He came into this not knowing what was going on. The other guide betrayed him.

Of course, Miles said. **Betrayal from within.**

Ryker looked down at Manila, and, for his own sake and

hers, he would check on Pablo. "You stay here," he told her. "I'll see what condition he's in."

"What if he's past saving?"

"I don't know. What would you like me to do?"

With tears in her eyes, and he could see how difficult this was for her, she said, "You need to finish him then, before the wild animals come in and tear him apart."

"We'll see," he said. And he quickly slipped his way down the tree, checking to make sure nobody was around. And once he hit the pathway, he raced toward the river.

There, off to the side, was the young man. Pablo. His leg was bent awkwardly off to the side. He'd been hobbling on it before but not doing so well, and now he had multiple lacerations, bringing fresh blood to the surface.

Ryker bent at his side and realized none of the cuts were deep, but they were bleeding pretty rapidly. He washed them with river water, then took off his shirt, thankful he had another long-sleeved but lighter-weight shirt underneath, and ripped it up, binding the wounds that he could, while the young man stared up at him. "If you can stay quiet," Ryker said, "I might be able to save you."

"They did this to me," Pablo whispered.

"I know. And the other guide probably betrayed you."

Pablo nodded. "Old Man Alejandro. I'd heard rumors, but I didn't believe it, and I needed the money."

Ryker bandaged the young guide's wounds as best he could. Then he quickly raced to the river, scooped up more water and rinsed more blood off the young man. "We need to get you out of here," he said.

Pablo slowly stepped to his feet and said, "My leg's injured."

"Hang on while I get a crutch," Ryker said, pushing

Pablo to sit again. Ryder headed back to the jungle, tapping out a message to Miles. By the time Ryker had a crutch constructed for Pablo, Ryker came across another stick that he quickly used as a splint to keep Pablo's leg in the right position. "I don't know if it's broken or just dislocated, but we have to immobilize it so that you're not putting pressure on all the wrong joints." And he quickly set it right—causing Pablo to gasp in surprise—then bound the stick to his injured leg and once again helped him to his feet. Then he placed the crutch under his armpit and asked, "Now, can you move?"

Surprised, the young man took several steps and turned and smiled. "It's much better. Thank you."

"You'll still find the pain to be pretty bad," he said, "but I put the leg back into place." As Ryker turned around, Miles and the two male team members stood there.

"We have to leave here, and we'll cross the river to throw them off," Miles said.

"I'll get Manila," Ryker said. He left the three men with Miles and raced back to the tree. By the time he clambered back up, she sat there, waiting for him.

"Are they all down there?" she asked.

He nodded. "We have to go fast." He shouldered his packs and hers and then looked at her and sighed. He slipped one pack to the other side to give her one, and then told her to get on his back. Awkwardly moving as quietly as he could, but knowing he raised a ton of noise, he made his way down to the ground and lowered her to her feet, then raced with her at his side to the river.

The men studied the river, when the older one, Benjamin, said, "We can't cross that."

Ryker looked at it, checked upstream, and said, "More

rocks are up there."

"Just means we'll hit more rocks when we go under," Benjamin said.

Ryker led the way and turned to see Miles swing the young guide up in his arms, telling him, "It's better to save your strength for what you can do," he told the guide when the man opened his mouth. "These rocks will be much worse."

Ryker made it to where the river was wider. Most people went to where it was narrower, but then it meant a faster-moving current. A wider water surface meant it would take more time and effort to cross but at a slower-moving current. He looked at the two men and asked, "Do you think you can cross this?"

Andy nodded bravely. "I think so. I can swim well. But then, once I go under, I don't know. We're fully clothed."

"No choice," Ryker said. Then he looked at Manila. "What about you?"

"I'm good," she said as she struck out ahead of him, standing close to the bigger rocks.

The danger of that was the fact that the current once again wrapped around the rocks with the intent of pulling her off. He motioned for her to go where it was flatter and wider. She followed his lead, and it took about twenty minutes to get them across, but then Miles was still strug-gling to move with the young guide in his arms. Ryker stepped back halfway and held out his arms.

"We're okay," Miles said with a shake of his head. "Just show me where the better footing is. I can hardly see."

With that, Ryker guided Miles across. When they were all on the other side, Ryker said, "Get into the greenery first, and then we can talk." Safely on the other side, they stopped and glanced back at the river.

"How long before somebody comes in from the scent of blood?" Andy asked.

"Too soon. We can't stop here," Miles said.

"And, if we're really unlucky, they are already on our trail," Ryker said.

They continued making their way farther inland, before Benjamin complained, "Stop. I need a break. Besides, where are we going?"

"To a pickup point," Ryker said.

"What kind of a pickup?" Andy asked.

"Hopefully a helicopter."

"Yes," Benjamin agreed. "Call for one now. What's the holdup?"

"We're deep into guerrilla territory. Our people are searching for a mostly abandoned area, free of the drug cartel and of the guerrillas, with a clearing to land in too, where they can pick us up without all of us being shot down midair—or causing a war between our countries."

"Tell them to look harder and faster," Benjamin grumbled.

Ryker glared at him. "If not, we'll head to the ocean and get a ride from there."

"We're heading to the ocean now," Manila said. "And I really want to stop and take a look at an outcropping of rocks up ahead."

Immediately Benjamin and Andy protested.

Ryker looked at her and asked, "What rock formation and what are you looking for?"

"It's one of the reasons I came to this region," she explained. "It wouldn't take long. I just need to scoop up a couple samples and take some photographs."

He stared at her in disbelief.

"Remember? I'm looking for platinum," she said. "The world's reserve is very low, and everybody is out looking for more."

"You'll have a hell of a time mining it here."

"Not my problem," she said with a shrug. "I'm the geologist. My job's just to find it."

"We'll see," Ryker said, but that's all he'd say. He wanted to ignore her request, but he knew that she would just as likely come back again—and on her own that time—if she didn't get a chance now. Or Global would send another whole team back, and that would put even more people in danger. "Do you know exactly where it is?"

"No, just a vague pointing in a general direction. But we sat and looked at the maps last night," she said. "And I figure it's a little bit farther in this direction. You just happened to be taking that direction as well to escape. And, therefore, I was thinking that, if we got the chance, it wouldn't be a problem." Her voice at the end was hopeful, entreating.

"Of course it's a problem. Don't listen to her," Benjamin snapped. "She's all about work."

"Of course. That's why I'm here," she said in a calm voice.

But Ryker could hear the tension in her voice. "That's not the point," he said. "Whenever you think you need to veer off, let me know. In the meantime, we're going straight forward and straight ahead. We're aiming for the coast. I think we have twenty-two miles to go."

The others groaned, whereas she nodded grimly and said, "Then we better get moving. I understand we'll have to spend another night out in the open at this rate. And that's not something I want to consider."

Ryker picked up the pace and headed forward.

CHAPTER 5

MANILA REALLY DID want to stop and see that rock formation, but she understood the others' point of view too. This would suck one way or the other, but it was much better if it were the safer way. She could feel sweat dripping down her back. They hadn't taken the opportunity to fill up their water bottles, and that was foolish. Then she realized that they were roughly following the water path anyway. So maybe they would fill up at any point in time. She took another sip from her bottle and kept on walking. They couldn't go too fast because of the injured guide. She looked back at him with a smile and asked, "Pablo, how are you doing?"

He gave her the briefest of smiles. "I'm alive, and that's more than I was a little bit ago, and, for that, I owe you."

"You owe Ryker," she said calmly. "But, then again, I wanted him to save you when those guys came after you. I didn't know what they would do to you."

"They talked about killing me right off the bat," he admitted, "but they thought it would be more fun for the animals and me if they just slashed me enough to bring lots of blood. That way the jungle animals could tear me apart alive. These guerrillas are not nice."

"War doesn't make anybody nice," Miles said from behind them both. "Now let's move it along faster."

At that, Pablo tried to move as fast as he could, but it wore him down. Moments later they came to a particularly rough spot of tree trunks and brush. Manila watched as Miles bent down and picked Pablo up. "I can't carry you the whole twenty-one miles," Miles said, "so I'll pick the spots where it's the worst for you."

Pablo nodded and whispered, "Thank you. Any help is much appreciated. I have my life again, and I don't want to lose it a second time."

"We don't intend to let you die," Miles said. "We didn't save you to lose you now."

With a smile and a half laugh, Manila turned and raced to where Ryker was leading. "You guys are just softies," she announced. He looked at her in horror, and she grinned and continued, "I get that you have this big tough-man image, but Miles is carrying Pablo again."

"He was slowing us down," Ryker said briefly.

"Sure," she said. "He was. But it wasn't that bad."

"There is no *that bad* here," he said. "We're surrounded by guerrillas and animal predators. We'll be under attack at any time. The sooner we get to the coast, the better."

"Do you really think we'll get there today?"

"It's only twenty-plus miles," he said.

"Oh, I hear you," she said, "but that's doable for you. Most of us aren't used to walking that distance in this heat or these conditions."

"Then you better get used to them," he said calmly.

She studied him and said, "You really mean that, don't you?"

His lips tilted. "Push it today, or spend another night in the jungle?"

She groaned. "Still a long walk."

"I know that," he said. "How about you?"

She turned to look at Andy, who was already sweating heavily. "Andy, do you need some water?"

He nodded, and she passed him her bottle. His gaze lit up. "I didn't realize you had that," he said.

"Ryker's got a canteen and another bottle too," she said.

Andy nodded. "Miles has a couple as well. I just didn't have one for myself." He finished the bottle and groaned. "Now that feels much better."

Her gaze locked on Benjamin next. "Benjamin, you okay?" He just glared at her and kept on going. She shrugged and turned to Andy. "He's always grumpy."

"Is he?" he asked. "I'm not sure, as I don't spend much time with him. This mood is much worse though."

"Sure, but the circumstances are much worse, too," she said with a smile. After that, it was just a case of putting one foot in front of the other. When Ryker, in the front, finally called for a break, she collapsed at his feet and said, "It's the only time I'll ever pass out at a guy's feet," then laid there, struggling for breath.

"We've just done six miles," he said, glaring down at her.

"Well, guess what? The next twelve will be that much harder to get through."

"I know," he said. He pulled out his spare bottle and handed it to her, then took the empty one from her. He dropped his bags and said, "I'll be back in a moment."

She had no idea where the river was now and was surprised when Ryker came back fifteen minutes later with fresh water. They all drank their fill and sat, trying to recuperate.

"Any idea if guerrillas are in this area?" Andy asked. "Because I really don't want to see any more."

Ryker turned to look at Pablo, who was sitting, his skin

pale, but he was drinking, and he was still conscious. "Pablo, do you know if any guerrilla camps are here?"

"No," he said. "You're off the main track. I know that much but not very much more. I don't know this area."

"And what about you?" Ryker asked, turning to Manila. "You didn't mention when you came to that formation."

"I know. I didn't see it," she admitted. She sat here, studying the area around them for a while. "But I would like a rock from there." She pointed to the left of the path. There, the path opened up with almost no greenery and just more rock upon rock. She stood and took several hesitant steps in that direction but heard a slithering sound that made her heart freeze.

Instantly Ryker was at her side. He had a machete in his hand.

She carefully looked down to see something yellow slithering across her boot. "Oh, God," she said. "I really don't like snakes."

"You're in the wrong line of work then," he said, as they waited for the snake to slip into the nearby brush.

Ryker walked with her several dozen yards ahead, and, when they exited the green area, he could see the formation she was talking about. "Tell me what rock you want," he said.

"I want ones with a little bit of white and some dark." Manila moved forward, studying them, her attention completely on the rocks around her now. There, she spied one that caught her eye. She reached down and picked it up and said, "This one's good." She added it to her pack and quickly wrote something down in her notes. "The location," she said. "You have a GPS? I need the location where we're at."

Once he told her, she smiled and wrote it down and then looked around more. "This one looks interesting."

He touched her arm and pulled lightly. "Come on," he said. "Let's return to the others."

"Can't I go up here and get a few more?"

He glared at her.

She frowned. "What's one more rock?"

"Twelve more miles," he countered.

She frowned.

He sighed and said, "Fine. You can pick *one* more rock."

She instantly pointed to the right and said, "I want one of those."

He walked over to where she pointed and picked up a fairly small one. "How about this?"

"That works," she said. "It doesn't have to be super big, but I do have to see what the content is in order to determine if any platinum is in there."

"How does that work?"

And she launched into a geological explanation that she could see immediately had his eyes glazing over. "Sorry," she said. "I tend to get very enthusiastic about my work."

"Enthusiasm's fine," he said. "It's just a little bit too much technical stuff right away."

She laughed. "Good point," she said. "Let's join the others."

And, with her new rocks, she headed back toward the others. She found them collapsed in the shade. It looked like Andy was sound asleep. She frowned. "Is he okay?"

"He's not used to the heat," Miles said.

"Right. None of us really are," she apologized.

"And yet, you're out here, wandering off into the forest."

"Of course," she said. "It's work."

"Fools," Benjamin said.

"You're a fine one to talk," she said in exasperation. "This is what you do too."

"Yeah, but I just decided this is my last trip," he said. "The last thing I need is to come up against guerrillas."

She glanced at Pablo. "How're you doing, Pablo?"

He smiled at her. "I'm okay," he said. "As long as I'm not dripping blood and leaving a trail, we'll be okay."

She stared at him in horror as she thought about that. "Are you dripping blood at all?"

He shook his head. "No. It's all good."

"So says you," Benjamin said. "Jesus."

"It's not his fault," Manila said, rounding on him.

Benjamin shrugged. "They are his own people."

"I hardly think the guerrillas are his own people," she said in Pablo's defense.

"Come to think of it, I wonder where the other guide is. Did they beat him up too?" Pablo asked.

"Meaning that Alejandro could have been killed or nearly so and tossed into the bush?" she asked, studying his face.

Pablo was visibly upset at her suggestion, but he nodded. "Well, that's not quite what I meant, but I guess that'll do."

She smiled. "Well, let's hope that didn't happen because, at least, if he betrayed us, maybe the guerrillas would keep him alive."

"They will," Pablo said. "I think he's done this often."

"Why would he do something like that?"

"He helps them to keep strangers away."

"And gets paid for it?" she asked. She looked at Miles and Ryker, but neither looked surprised. "Is everybody just out for themselves?"

"Absolutely," Ryker said. "That's one of the biggest lessons you should learn right off the bat."

"I'm not of that mindset," she said. "Surely there is another way to look at the world and not be quite so jaded." She studied the small lines at the corner of Ryker's mouth and the frown creasing his forehead. Then she sighed and nodded. "You've seen so much of the darker side of life. You need to spend some time with the lighter side."

"Lighter side?" he asked in amusement.

She shrugged. "Family outings and parties and friendly stuff, like a day at the beach, and not a day in a guerrilla-warfare nightmare."

"When we get out of here," he said, "I'll consider your offer."

She stared at him in surprise. "Offer?" she asked hesitantly.

Miles laughed. "Your invitation to spend the day with him at the beach."

She thought about it and shrugged. "What the hell. Why not? You both need to do something other than this." She motioned at the world around them.

"What about you?" Ryker asked. "This is what you're doing."

"But not for very long at a time," she said. "This is a couple of weeks out of my life. But I think, for you, the beach is a couple weeks out of your life whereas *this* is your life."

"Interesting," Miles said, looking at her curiously. "It's almost like you know him."

"Well, I don't know that I understand him well," she said, "but you can tell that his life hasn't been easy."

"It doesn't matter about my life," Ryker said. "We must get going again. And moving much faster. Are you guys ready?" He looked at the group collapsed around him and frowned. "These miles won't eat themselves up on their own."

"Maybe not," Benjamin said, "but resting is a hell of a lot easier on our bodies." Just then came a slithering and a hissing sound close to him. He bolted to his feet and swore as a large snake crept up the tree beside him. "Jesus, I hate this place," he said, hopping around on his feet and stomping his boots.

"It didn't get into your boot," Manila said. "Stop making a big deal out of it."

"So says you," he snapped, his attitude turning downright vicious. "For all I know, you sent that damn thing my way anyway."

Hurt, she stared at him in shock. "You know I would never do something like that," she stated. "Why would you even say that?"

Andy looked at Benjamin, puzzled. "Hey, no need for personal attacks," he said, rubbing the sleep out of his eyes as he stood up. "You didn't have to come on this trip."

"No, I didn't have to," he said, "but I had to because it's the job I was offered. So I took it. We're not all allowed to just pick and choose the jobs we want."

"So maybe it's time for you to retire," Miles said, studying him.

She looked at Benjamin and then back at Miles and Ryker, not sure what was going on. "Seriously? Are you considering retiring?"

Benjamin groaned and said, "Well, I would if I could, but I can't afford to. But I'm not coming back to this godforsaken place again." He turned and looked at Ryker. "Isn't it time to start moving? I just want to go home."

Ryker nodded and motioned toward Pablo. "You ready?"

The young man grimaced and said, "As much as I'll ever be. If I can't go with you guys, I'm dead anyway. So I need to keep up somehow." He got on his feet again and picked up the crutch and hopped his way forward.

Manila was amazed at how well he was handling this scenario as it was. Because, for her, it was a whole lot worse to maneuver on crutches. "You're doing really well, Pablo."

He shook his head. "No. I wish I could walk."

"Try the leg," Ryker said. "With that dislocation back in place, it might not be too bad now."

Pablo put his weight on his foot and nodded. "I can put weight on it," he said excitedly. "Could walk faster, except for the splint."

At that, Miles reached down and slashed the material holding this splint in place. "Try that."

Pablo walked around and said, "Well, I'll probably collapse by the end of the day, and I probably will have damaged the knee, but I can walk much better this way." He carried the crutch with him just in case and then bent and picked up the ties they had used—just in case as well. "Let's go."

Manila hopped to her feet, smiled and said, "Now that's much better. Come on then. Off to the beach we go."

And she fell into place behind Ryker.

RYKER SMILED AS she appeared to be buoyant and happy. Nobody else gave a shit, although Pablo was doing very well holding his own. The guerrillas had left the guide more or less for dead, but his cuts weren't deep. Just running blood. Was that inexperience on their part, or was that intentional to bring in the predators here? Or was Pablo a trap?

Ryker sure hoped not, but it wouldn't surprise him anymore. He just had to keep an eye on everybody. All it would take was for someone to slow them down so the guerrillas could lay a trap ahead.

Just then his comm tapped, Miles warning him of exactly the same thing. It was sad when you had to worry that the person you had rescued was a Trojan horse, trying to get into the group to betray you all over again. But no doubt that was a possibility they would have to deal with.

Ryker quickly set a pace, grueling but doable, hoping that everybody would eat up a few more miles. He was afraid, at this stage, they wouldn't make it as far as they needed to. The last thing he wanted was to get stuck in the jungle one more night with this lot. But he was pretty damn sure it would be at least one more. He just hoped it wouldn't be more than that.

CHAPTER 6

MANILA STRUGGLED TO keep up behind Ryker. Miles had been sent up a tree to scout ahead, then out at a fast run in front of them to further investigate the area. Meanwhile, Ryker had taken the lead—demanding that Benjamin take his post behind all the rest—and, as soon as they reached a heavy foliage area, Ryker brought up machetes, one in each hand, to carve a path forward.

It meant there was absolutely no way to hide the trail in the jungle they had made and then took, but it was the only way, as far as they were concerned, to get closer to the coast. It appeared to be an old path along here. But, short of crawling on the ground, a large section of it was almost impossible to pass. Manila had to admit, she was sweating heavily.

But Ryker appeared to just throw it off and not care. His gaze searched unceasingly.

She didn't know how he could just keep going. The stamina and endurance required were unbelievable. It made it a lot easier though with Pablo able to keep up. He was doing much better now that the splint was off his leg. From a commonsense point of view, he should be off his leg as much as possible, but that didn't appear to be an option right now. The men couldn't possibly carry him all the way, but, as Pablo still moved forward at a much slower pace than her team, she realized that they would definitely spend another night in the jungle. And that wasn't something she looked forward to.

When she heard Ryker swear all of a sudden, she glanced up at him, and abruptly his arm swept out and pulled her backward. She watched a huge snake slide off one of the branches directly into their path, its tongue flicking out, tasting the air all around it as it homed in on its next prey. She sucked in her breath and whispered, "God, I'm starting to hate this place."

He shot her an amused look. "Anything other than rocks not thrill you?"

"Rocks are always much better," she said. "I like things that are hard all the time."

As soon as she let the words slip out, heat shot over her cheeks. She refused to look at Ryker, even though she knew he stared at her with an interested gaze. She motioned at the snake in front of her. "That's one I don't know. I have no intention of getting bit by it."

"None of us are," he said.

She watched as it dropped to the ground and slithered into the deep underbrush. "You need to warn the others."

"Oh, we know," Andy said. "You can bet Pablo and Benjamin already know too."

They slowly walked past where the snake had been, and she realized that all it did was remind her that the snakes were everywhere. Many thousands of them were in this part of the world. The one that had dropped down in front of her just brought to mind how hundreds more were right around her, staying out of sight, but could strike at any moment. Although a ton of pythons and anacondas were here as well, they weren't so much about striking as much as grabbing on and squeezing. She wasn't sure which would be a worse way to die, but, in any case, she didn't want to have a second close-up encounter with that reptile in particular. She looked at Ryker to see him wiping the sweat off his forehead. "You okay?"

"I'm okay," he said. "But it'll be slow progress if we can't find another route through here. Do you want to talk to Pablo to see if he knows his area at all?"

"I did," she said. "It's all new territory for him."

"Figures," he said as he brought up a machete again. "This next section isn't quite so dense though. Let's get through it." And they moved forward again.

She almost didn't want to raise her foot and follow him. Every muscle in her body ached. She wondered how much of that was the lack of water and food or just the lack of rest. She knew that tomorrow would be bad, but no way would she complain because they had to keep going. They had no other option.

Finally, after another hour, Ryker slowed down and looked back at the others. "How are you holding up?"

Andy surprisingly nodded and said, "I'm doing okay."

Ryker looked at Benjamin, who shrugged instead of being difficult. He had gone quiet.

"How are you doing back there with Pablo?" he called out as loudly as he safely could.

"I'm moving," Benjamin said. "We've been at this for hours."

"Absolutely, and it'll be hours more."

They all turned and headed toward the same pathway that he had carved for them. But it was distracting because, once the thought of a break had entered their minds, the whole group thought about it. She'd seen it happen time and time again. "We need to get another mile in," she said to her team and kept up behind Ryker.

He was right. This section was less dense. It was a lot easier as it went by. She could bend and push branches back and forth and manage to quickly move several hundred yards forward. Just as she considered that maybe they would be okay for the next while though, he grabbed her shoulder and pulled her back. He had his hand to his earpiece. She turned to him in surprise, and he immediately clapped a hand over her mouth. The others behind them were all frozen in place. She looked up at Ryker, and he motioned in front of them. He bent and put his mouth against her ear and whispered, "People."

Instantly, she froze and snuggled close to him. He wrapped his arms around her and held her tight. She could feel the shakes setting in. The very last thing she wanted in her world right now was to get captured again. And she knew that the last time would be easy compared to the next time. She wanted to ask him a million questions but knew that no way could she make a sound.

She heard laughter in the distance, and the sounds of many feet as they trampled forward. She twisted slightly to look up at him, but his ear was cocked, as if trying to figure out where they were traveling to and from. And, of course, that was important because, if a path was up ahead, then Ryker and company needed to utilize it as much as they could.

What they couldn't afford to do would be to choose a path where the guerrillas would likely come back through. They also didn't know how many guerrillas there were or where they were all heading.

Ryker pulled out a compass. He checked his bearings

here and nodded, then tucked it back into his pocket. Manila had been following along herself on their own variants to make sure that they were heading in the right direction, but it was frustrating to know that a pathway was here that could handle at least ten people or maybe even twenty. The thought of an even bigger group of guerrillas made her insides curl.

She could barely breathe for the humidity; several bugs worked around her face, and she didn't even move. If they wanted a chunk out of her, they would take it, and there wasn't a whole lot she could do to stop it.

Just as one landed on her forehead, Ryker reached up and pinched it between his fingers and killed it. She shot him a grateful smile, and then he urged her forward and said, "I'll go first." Then he slipped past her but hung onto her hand. They watched in the distance as a large group of guerrillas carried on away from them. Their path originated from the right. He checked the direction of their path and said, "Well, we have a couple choices. We can follow behind them and possibly meet up with more of them or we can go in the opposite direction."

"Meaning, we go our own path?"

He nodded. "I wouldn't want to use their path at all. Anybody who can read trails will see that we came this way. Our footwear is very different from theirs."

She glanced down at her boots and nodded. "Then we keep doing what we're doing."

But he studied the path and said, "It branches off up here." In fact, they stared at what was a very heavily traveled path, almost like a small road in front of them. But this better path crossed from left to right, and the guerrillas had gone left, whereas Ryker pointed out a continuation of the path they were on that branched off ahead.

She nodded. "As long as it continues where we need to go." And, with that, they quickly crossed the well-traveled path and moved off on the tangent that went into the deeper brush. And seeing those guerrillas so close by, nobody was looking to stay here.

When Ryker finally came to another stop, his gaze was alert and aware. Manila marveled once again at how much he managed to do. She struggled just to stay up with him and Miles and knew that Pablo behind her would be really struggling. She turned to the stragglers in line to see Pablo getting a break on this last section from Miles.

"When did Miles rejoin us?" she asked Ryker.

He only grinned.

She looked between Miles and Ryker. "Is everybody okay?" she asked in a low voice.

"Yes, but we'll take a twenty-minute break," Ryker said. "Up here." And he motioned toward a set of large flat rocks. A lot of greenery was all around it, but there were places to sit.

Manila scrambled up to the top of one and slowly collapsed. "It might be a mistake to stop though," she groaned as she shuffled her body so that she lay on her back, with her feet completely relaxed.

"Maybe," he said, handing her water. "But we need to give our muscles a bit of rest too, so they can fight better when we need them to."

"Says you," she says. "You're Superman. Me? I'm feeling very much less than Wonder Woman."

Andy chuckled as he sat down beside her. "Hey, we're doing okay so far." He glanced at Ryker. "How far do you figure we've gone?"

"That's the reason for the break," he said. "We're halfway."

Everybody stared at him in shock and then groaned.

Ryker nodded. "We still have another good twelve miles to go."

Andy dropped his head into his arms and sighed as he said, "We can do it. It's just the heat and the humidity."

"Exactly," Ryker said. Then he looked down at her and asked, "Do you have any food?"

She winced and shook her head. "I only have my work backpack. We lost our bags." She looked at Andy. "They took your bags too, didn't they?"

He lifted his shirt to show his little belt pack. "They left my camera, which I thought was odd, but whatever. It's the most expensive thing I brought with me," he said. Then he reached down and continued, "I do have a little bit of gum." He brought it out and carefully passed it around for everybody to have one. He put the empty package away.

"There's got to be something to eat on the trail." Ryker glanced at Pablo. "What food could we find here?"

It was about twenty minutes later that Pablo pointed out several trees with edible fruits. Ryker cut down several, following Pablo's directions to test for the ripest of the fruits; they all indulged in soft and juicy maracuyá fruits.

Manila loved the flavor, but it was the moisture she found herself constantly biting for.

When everybody had eaten their fill, Ryker looked at them and said, "Sorry, it's time to get going again. Next time we stop, we'll be halfway from here to there."

"And how long will that take?"

"At this rate, at least three hours. Unless we can pick up the pace …"

At that, she hopped to her feet and said, "Well, nothing'll solve this problem if we sit here."

Just then Benjamin let out a shriek. He hopped off the stone to reveal a very small bug scrambling past.

"Did it bite you?" Ryker snapped.

Benjamin looked at Ryker in shock, his hands immediately checking, and he shook his head, gasping, "No, no, I don't think so."

"Well, you'd know," Ryker said. "If not now, within five minutes. That was a special Colombian scorpion, and you'll be dead soon, so, if you have any bites, you need to tell me."

"No." Benjamin shook his head. "God, I want to go home. I want to go home before something in here kills me."

"We all want to go home," Manila said. "We're doing our best to get there."

"Says you," he said. "You're the one who wanted to be here."

"I wanted to be where the rocks were," she corrected. "I wasn't planning on trekking across the jungle like this, escaping many groups of guerrillas."

"Well, that's why we hired the local guides, isn't it?" Andy asked, looking at Pablo. But he looked a whole lot worse for wear. "I don't know if he'll make another twelve miles," Andy said in a worried tone.

She winced, not sure Pablo would either. His skin had taken on an odd color. She looked at Miles to see him staring back at her, his gaze flat. He already knew that Pablo's chances were slim. He was willing to give it his all to give him an out, but she could see it already. If they couldn't get to the coast and if Pablo didn't get medical attention soon, Pablo wouldn't make it at all.

RYKER KEPT MOVING the group forward. He knew their odds of getting to the coast unscathed were slim, but he was willing to take every chance he could to get them there. Pablo was a bigger concern. Not only would it be hard to keep him up and moving, but he also needed medical attention that was likely already too late to save him. Ryker didn't know what was going on with his system and whether the guerrillas had put something into his cuts, but Pablo's energy was fading, and his color wasn't good. Ryker and Miles had exchanged a few quiet words on his condition.

As soon as they got to the next fresh water source, Ryker would clean out Pablo's wounds again and see if they could do something else for Pablo. But, short of having any medical facilities, only so much was available in this part of the world.

He didn't know these native plants in terms of his own wilderness survival skills as much as he did those in the US and Canada. The plants here were foreign and vaster in variety. He had hoped that Pablo himself would know, but apparently, he was on his very first trip as a jungle guide, and that just made him dangerous. A little bit of knowledge was deadly. About half an hour in, Ryker switched places with Miles to lead the group, while Ryker stayed at the back with Pablo. As they moved forward with him urging Pablo along, he asked, "Why did you come on this trip then?"

"My uncle urged me to," he said.

"Is this what you wanted to do?"

Pablo shrugged. "Many people in the village do it, so I wasn't against doing it."

"But your uncle thought you should do it?"

"Yes, but then I was also in the way and just one more mouth to feed, when I should be bringing in money," he said. "It's normal."

"Of course it is," Ryker said. "And do most of the tour guides do very well?"

"Most of them," he said. "At least the seasoned ones."

"And the unseasoned ones?"

"Some come back. Some get caught by the guerrillas. Some are made to join the guerrillas. It's hard to say."

"And were you expecting that to happen to you?"

"No," he gasped out as he landed wrong on the uneven path in front of him. "But I think my uncle was hoping I would."

And that just confirmed what Ryker was thinking. "Did he have any connection to the older guide, Alejandro?"

"They were friends," he said. "That's one of the reasons I got this opportunity. He would show me the ropes and help me to gain some experience."

"And do you feel he did that?"

Pablo shot him a look. "Right now, I'm thinking my uncle paid him something to have me not come back," he snapped.

"Glad to hear your brain is working properly at least," Ryker said smoothly, "because that's what I'm thinking too."

Pablo's face was grim. "I'm also not sure that the guerrillas didn't do something else besides slicing me open pretty good," he said. "My belly is on fire."

Ryker lifted Pablo's shirt in an instant and said, "I'm looking for fresh water so we can wash your wounds again."

"There's some sap we need," Pablo said. "If we could find it, I can put it on the wounds, and it will help."

"Keep your eye out for it."

"I have been," Pablo said. "The tree grows closer to the water though."

"Some fresh water should be coming up. We've been following the creek as it crisscrossed our path. It should be coming back around again soon."

Pablo nodded. "I hope it's soon enough."

So did Ryker, but he didn't want to say it out loud. He heard a shout up ahead, and, of course, that would be Manila. He tapped his comm.

Miles said, "We have a creek coming up."

"Good. Everybody needs to fill up with water, and we need to wash Pablo's wounds."

"Exactly. And I think I see one of the sap-bearing trees that we need for his wounds too."

"Did you talk to him about it?" Ryker asked Miles.

"Yes," Miles said. "I've been looking all along, but I haven't seen it since we first left. But I think this is it."

Ryker urged Pablo forward and said, "We think we found the tree sap you're looking for." And as soon as they came up to the creek, the water rushing past the air visibly lightened. Ryker took a moment and took several deep breaths of fresh air, loving the light and clean moisture here. He looked at the others as they soaked their heads, washed their arms and faces, just trying to cool down. Even as he watched, Manila took a bottle of water and poured it under her shirt along her chest and her back. He understood the sentiment. They took the time to stop, even though it wasn't the location that he wanted to push forward to, because, given Pablo's condition, it was necessary.

With Pablo stretched out on the ground and resting, Ryker quickly unwrapped the crude bandages that he had used. Then he handed them off to Manila, so she can rinse them in the cold water, while Miles and Andy collected the sap they needed. Although Pablo's cuts weren't deep slices, the edges of the wounds were puffy and angry. Ryker rinsed them, and then they quickly placed the sap along the edge of each and every one. There were seven in all. He shook his head and wondered at the cruelty. None of them were deep, but they were all at places that would cause a great deal of pain.

With all of the sap now covering the open wounds, Ryker did his best to rebandage them. And then he helped Pablo off with his T-shirt. Manila took the shirt to the river and quickly rinsed and wrung it out and then brought it back. In the meantime, they washed his torso down, trying to reduce as much of his fever as possible. When helping him to sit up to put the T-shirt back on, Ryker saw the slice in his jeans. "Did they cut your leg?"

Pablo looked at him in confusion.

Ryker could see the fever building in his gaze. He motioned at Pablo's leg. "It looks like your leg is cut. Is it?"

Pablo stared down at it but didn't seem to comprehend.

Ryker was already pulling apart the cut edges of his jeans to see the blood and, indeed, something puffy and nasty-looking. He swore at that and took his knife, then cut the jean leg open a little bit more so that he could expose the area of the wound. It was more of a stab instead of a slash.

They quickly cleaned it, while Pablo cried out in pain, but this was the one causing most of Pablo's problems. It took several trips and another shirt donated by Miles to clean out the wound and then to cut it into strips for bandages but not before they liberally covered this wound in the sap. And, with that, Ryker tied the leg wound up tight again, using part of the T-shirt as a bandage and then part of it to wrap around Pablo's leg and said, "That's the wound we have to keep an eye out for."

Pablo nodded. "That would explain why I'm feeling so bad," he muttered.

"Well, you're getting a fever," Ryker said. "That's not helping how you feel either. Unfortunately, we can't stay here. We have to keep moving."

Pablo, immediately terrified that they would leave him behind, struggled to his feet. "I can make some more miles," he said in broken English.

"You could," Ryker said. "But I think, for the moment, you're better off if we carry you." He motioned to Miles and said, "Take up the lead again. I'll bring up the rear with Pablo." They watched as he took several vines and laced them up under his thighs and around his butt, then around his waist while Pablo stared at him in surprise.

"What are you doing?"

"Just in case you lose consciousness," Ryker said, "I need a harness to hold you on my back." Pablo wasn't small by any means, but he certainly was dwarfed by Ryker's size, and, within a very short time, Ryker had Pablo on his back, with the vines holding him half suspended in a harness.

Then Ryker waved the others on and said, "I can do this for a couple miles. Let's keep up the pace and get as far as we can. If we can reach the coast tonight, it'll be a whole different story tomorrow." And, with that, they headed down the same path again, this time following the trail across the creek and back over.

He wasn't sure how much longer they still had to go though, as he'd lost a little bit of his time here, but he also knew they couldn't afford to waste any more time either. Pablo didn't have that time. They were fighting as it was to keep him alive. "Pablo," Ryker said, "while you're conscious, you need to tell us about other plants to help bring down your fever. Anything that your tribes know about here to help you."

"I've been trying," Pablo gasped. "I know this one's for the slices. There's another one that we can make a tea from too, but not until we stop." He pointed out some branches just off to the side. It was from a little plant near the ground.

Ryker bent carefully with Pablo still on his back, and, between the two of them, they pulled as much of it as they could. Pablo immediately popped some of the leaves into his mouth. "If I chew it," he said. "That will help too."

"Do you have enough?" Ryker asked, straightening up and shifting the weight on his back.

"For now, yes. And, if I can save some, we'll make tea, and I can soak the leaves in the water. But otherwise, I'll keep doing what I'm doing."

"Okay, let's go then," Ryker said. "I know this will likely hurt, but I need to pick up the pace. We've fallen behind." He started to run as soon as he said that, and he could hear Pablo groan almost immediately. But Ryker had to ignore it. If there was one thing worse than being in the jungle like this with a wounded man, it was being separated from the others. Ryker couldn't afford to let that happen at any cost. He kept bolting through the trees, ducking and moving as fast as he could as he tried to catch up to the others, who were now at least one hundred to maybe two hundred yards in front of him, but they were definitely out of sight.

CHAPTER 7

MANILA STOPPED WHEN she couldn't see any sign of Ryker behind her. She wanted to call out, but she didn't dare because she didn't want to let anybody else in the vicinity know where they were. As she stopped in place, Andy reached out and grabbed her hand.

"Come on," he said in a low whisper.

"There's no sign of Ryker and Pablo," she said, resisting Andy's urge to go forward.

Up ahead, Miles said, "Forget about them. Ryker has got this in hand." Then he tapped the comm device in his ear. Relieved, Manila nodded and turned and fell into place behind Andy. But still, she kept turning to look behind. When she thought to bring it up with Miles again, she heard a heavy *thump*. As she turned, Ryker ran toward them, catching up, even with Pablo on his back. She could feel the relief settling inside her.

As soon as he reached them, she kept up, just staying ahead of him to make sure that she didn't slow him down. "You had me worried," she hissed.

"We're fine," he said.

She glanced at Pablo to see him smiling at her briefly, and she nodded. "Good thing. The terrain up ahead looks rough."

"All the terrain is rough," he said. "This was the best

route that we could figure out."

"When did you figure that out?" she asked.

"Before we even left and landed in the jungle," he said.

She stared at him, startled, and he nodded. "You never go into a scenario if you don't have a way out again. At least one. If not three or four."

She thought about that and realized that it was more than just common sense. That was a survival instinct which she didn't appear to have any experience with. Even though she had traveled all around the world to various geological locations for rocks, she hadn't had any experience with something like this. She'd always had helicopters, telecommunication, support people and teams available. Well, the good news here was, this team was on her side. The bad news was, they didn't have helicopters to pick them up from the jungle.

"How will we get off the shore?" she asked.

"By boat," he said succinctly.

"Do you have one waiting for us?" she asked hopefully.

He shook his head. "Not like you mean."

She didn't know what that meant either. He wasn't exactly forthcoming in his comments. He'd answer every question, but he wouldn't volunteer anything. But then she realized the amount of effort he expended carrying Pablo. Pablo had to be at least a hundred and twenty pounds. When she realized she had slowed her steps, of course, that was keeping them behind too. She immediately walked as fast as she could to catch up, knowing that Ryker would match her steps and stay with her.

As soon as she caught up with the others, she watched Benjamin glare at her. She shrugged. "I stopped to make sure they were okay."

"They're fine," he said. "And, if they slow us down too much, we'll have to leave them behind."

"We'll hardly do that," she said, glaring at him. "They came to save us."

"They also know how hard this rescue would be. They knew what they were getting into."

"*He* knew what he was getting into, you mean," she snapped. "This is only about Ryker."

"That's not the point. People have jobs all over the world where they help others. He's hardly unaware of all the possible outcomes."

"That doesn't mean we ditch them at the first sign of trouble that they run into."

"Whatever," Benjamin said. "I'm going home, and I'm staying home."

"It sounds like a good thing," Andy said. "What we don't want is this to be a case of losing our humanity and what makes us special, all due to hardships where we turn on each other."

She agreed with that. She hadn't really seen Benjamin as somebody who would be a deserter. But then he wasn't much of a team player either, so that made sense. He hadn't been her choice on this trip, but one of Global's owners had insisted. She guessed he'd had a ton of experience but none down in Colombia. She really wished she had a couple Colombian-experienced geologists. But then the tour guides were supposed to be that for her team, and one had betrayed them, while the other one was injured. And she wouldn't leave Pablo behind, no matter what Benjamin said.

The fact that Ryker was going above and beyond to keep Pablo safe showed just what kind of a man he was, and that brutally highlighted what kind of man Benjamin was. She couldn't imagine seeing two more different specimens of males at the same time.

She wasn't sure exactly where Andy fell in that spectrum now, but she thought a lot more honor was within him as he kept siding to save Pablo. She also knew that the longer this trek kept going, the harder it would be on Benjamin, and it would show his uglier side faster. Nothing like the veneer of society falling away when they were in a jungle like this, where it became a fight for survival, and the real people on the inside showed up.

She was happy for Andy though because he appeared to be the right kind of people. Miles and Ryker too, she already knew were the right kind. Only Benjamin showed himself to be so much less than she had hoped for. She could also see the darkness of night settling in deeper. And she realized just then that, no matter what they wanted, they couldn't avoid staying another night in the open air.

When Ryker caught up with her the next time, she said in a low voice, "Any idea how far we still have to go?"

"No," he said. "Well, I'm estimating somewhere around seven miles."

"It'll be dark soon," she murmured.

"We still have a couple hours of light to go," he said.

"Oh," she said. "Do you think so?"

Pablo spoke up. "It falls more rapidly on this side of the country," he said. "So we have about an hour and a half."

"So, we will put every moment of that to good use," Ryker said, motioning to her. "Go, go, go. Some parts of the jungle are fine, and some parts of it are much less fine."

She nodded and used the last of her energy to catch up with the others. She had hoped by now that the others would be long gone on this part of the trip. But no such luck. They were just ahead. "We can't keep going too long," she warned Ryker.

"We can keep going much longer than you think," Ryker replied. His voice was calm. "You never really know what you can do until you're in the situation where you're forced to do it."

She groaned at that. "That's not what I want to hear."

"Doesn't matter," he said. "This is the scenario we have. We could come across more guerrillas at any moment."

Almost like his words were prophetic, no sooner had he said that when an odd whistle came from Miles up in front. She froze and looked back at Ryker. He frowned, and he grabbed her, and all three hid in the brush.

"What's going on?" she whispered.

Immediately he placed a finger against her lips and gave her a hard look. She pinched her lips together and waited. She heard footfalls, quiet and stealthy. She realized it was the guerrillas, and she slowly sagged to the ground, desperate to hide farther and deeper into the underbrush. But Ryker had a problem. He was carrying Pablo, and, although Pablo was as quiet as he could be, Ryker couldn't hide himself or Pablo as easily.

But, being Ryker, he wasn't short on answers. Instead of going down as she had, he scrambled up and very quickly disappeared into the branches above. She could only hope that Benjamin and Andy were well hidden and that Miles was looking after them.

And, sure enough, two guerrillas walked past, their steps steady and purposeful, rifles at their sides slung over their shoulders. Whether they were looking for them or looking for something else, they headed in the opposite direction of where her team had come. Which meant that they should be aware very soon of the group's travels because of their very obvious trail.

Yet maybe the descending darkness would hide their tracks. And she knew that her group would immediately have to veer off the pathway and forge a new one. That would make their traveling even harder.

As soon as the pair of guerrillas were past them by several hundred yards, Ryker slipped down the tree and gathered Manila and moved as fast as he could forward to catch up to the others. They quickly then veered off into the densest part of the jungle.

She knew the snakes were everywhere, and she could just feel the predators' eyes watching them as they continued to slog for miles. They weren't on the main pathway or even an old pathway, so now it was truly hard going. She wished they could return to the more traveled path, but, every once in a while, they froze and stopped as people passed. Not close but close enough. Close enough that she knew they wouldn't get through the last few miles in any way but the hard way.

When Miles finally brought the group to a stop, she glanced around to see how everyone was doing. Benjamin had almost a glazed look in his eyes as he leaned against a rock. Andy had sagged to the ground right where he stood. She stared up at Miles. "How much farther?" She desperately wanted it to be the answer she wanted to hear, but Ryker answered her.

"We still have several more miles to go."

RYKER KNEW THE group was lagging badly. And, if it wasn't for the fact that they had come across several guerrillas out on hunting parties, he would have taken the slightly easier pathway rather than trying to forge their own way through the jungle. But they didn't dare.

He and Miles exchanged hard looks. Miles's gaze slipped to Pablo as he frowned. Ryker twisted slightly and whispered, "Pablo, you awake?" There was a slight groan which was almost a moan. It whispered through his lips. It dawned on Ryker that Pablo was slowly succumbing. Grim, Ryker looked at Miles and asked, "What do you think?"

Miles gave a hard shake of his head. "He's in bad shape."

"I know. How much farther?" He studied the light that they had.

"Maybe forty minutes of daylight left? But it's worse while we're at the end of our breath here. We can try diverting to a slightly easier path, but we might end up in a fight."

He contemplated what that would mean and then shrugged. "Still, might be easier."

"If it is, yes," Miles warned. "But if it's not?"

"We have to get to the coast," he said. "Otherwise, Pablo won't make it."

With that, Miles led the way to the closest slightly traveled path. Then they fell into line. Everybody was exhausted and pushed beyond their limit but still trudged along. Ryker watched as Manila forcibly tried to keep up. But she was sagging too. And he couldn't let her. He grabbed her arm and kept her with him, moving her forward with each step.

"I'm coming. I'm coming," she whispered in a hard voice.

"You can't be last," he said.

She nodded. "It's just so hard to keep up."

"No choice," he said. "Remember? We don't really know

who and what we are until we hit a particularly bad situation, and then we find out the truth."

"What if the truth is pretty ugly to admit to?" she whispered.

"It isn't," he said. "You have to keep digging deep."

She nodded and didn't even bother looking at him. "Maybe, but it's still hard."

"Of course it is," he said. "Everything in life worth doing is hard. Just think. In a couple days, you could be sitting back, curled up in bed with a cup of coffee, and I could be sitting beside you, wondering what all the fuss was about."

At that, her lips quirked, and she said, "I'll hold you to that."

"Will you?" he asked, curiosity spiking. "That would mean that I was seeing you first thing in the morning or had spent the night in bed with you and had gone out to get coffee early in the morning."

"I can see that happening," she said calmly.

His eyebrows shot up, and he studied her with interest. "Tell me more," he invited her.

She shook her head. "I so do not have the energy for that."

"True," he said, "but in a couple days …"

"In a couple days," she said, "I suspect we'll be in that bed together. But only if we make it that far."

"Oh, we'll make it," he said. "Just think of the extra incentive you just gave me."

She reached out and smacked him ever-so-lightly on his cheek and said, "There's an attraction between us that everyone else has already seen."

"If they've seen it, whatever," he said. "As long as they don't bother you about it. Just because there's a connection doesn't mean either of us is foolish enough to act on it."

"At least not here," she said with some spirit. And then, with a laugh that seemed to add an extra bounce to her step, she picked up the pace.

He watched her pull away, and he softly called out, "You won't get away that fast."

She sent him a saucy look. "But you still have to catch up. You'll never catch me if you're behind all the time."

He grinned at that. As long as the banter was harmless and kept her spirits up, he was all for it. The fact of the matter was, she was a hell of a specimen too. Not only was she physically long and lean but she was also fit, and her brain and heart were in the right place. Especially her heart. She kept checking to make sure that he was there with them.

He wasn't used to that. Even a SEALs team would have left him on his own to survive as they knew best. Not that they would have completely abandoned him by any means, but they would have waited for him to have caught up at the next station. And, if he hadn't shown up, then, yes, they would have come looking. But, in her case, she wasn't letting him get too far behind at all.

It was a novel idea, and one that he thoroughly enjoyed. But Pablo and the heat pouring off his body worried Ryker. He was already dealing with the dehydration and the jungle humidity of Colombia, but, with Pablo's weight on his back, Ryker felt like he was in a furnace. But he kept up, and they kept going faster and faster and deeper and deeper, and he knew every mile they got under their belt was another mile they wouldn't have to deal with.

And just when they were ready to take a break, there was a sudden shout in front. He heard Miles swearing. "Four," he said over the comm.

"Dammit." Ryker quickly raced ahead, getting Manila to hide by the end of the brush. He pulled up his firearm, and, as the first gunman leveled his rifle at Miles, Ryker picked him off. And, with the first shot fired, the guerrillas spread out. But that sent one in his direction. Ryker took him out quickly, and, as he raced forward, he picked up the guerrilla's weapon and headed to the next one.

Miles stood with his hands up, and two guerrillas angrily screamed in his face. Ryker came up from behind and, using the rifle butt, slammed one of the men on the side of the head. Miles took down the second one in the next instant.

Manila stood up, looked at him, and asked, "Did you kill those first two men?"

He looked at her and said, "If you point a gun, don't point it for any other reason."

She swallowed hard and nodded. "I guess there wasn't much choice, was there?"

He shook his head. "There wasn't. Now, check the bodies for water and food." He motioned as Miles was already running through the men on the ground, checking them for anything that they might have had. He took their weapons from them and did a thorough search but came up empty. "Then leave them where they are," Ryker continued. "These last two will wake up soon enough, but we'll have their guns. Still, we need to be long gone."

Now, with everybody heavily armed with rifles, Andy carrying two, Benjamin with one, even Manila holding one, they picked up the rest of the weapons and started to move.

This time Ryker took the lead. He ignored the burden on his back. He had packed several hundred pounds in his SEALs lifetime through rough terrain for many miles in any given day so many times anyway. Not in this humidity, he'd agree, but this wasn't the time to get fussy. He could feel the weight every time he landed, jarring up and down his spine. But, worse than that, he knew it sent an echo through the jungle.

As soon as he got close to a mile put between them and the latest guerrillas, Ryker slowed ever-so-slightly and turned his footsteps into much more silent steps as he glided through the jungle forest, knowing that Miles was pushing the others behind to keep up. As he glanced behind, Manila was right on his heels. He smiled at that. A path diverged up ahead, and he deliberately chose the one less traveled.

By the time he came to a slow stop, he figured he'd put a good two and a half miles between them and their latest guerrilla incident. He turned to wait for the others to catch up. When they did, he raised an eyebrow at Miles.

Miles just nodded and said, "Looks like we're clear."

"How can we be clear?" Andy asked. "The guerrillas are everywhere here. This is their turf. This is their terrain. Once they find their fallen friends, they'll be all over us."

"Yes," Ryker said, "which is why we have to keep going."

"Won't they have a base or something on the water?"

"There are towns," he said. "Yes. And they'll have eyes and ears everywhere. Spies and those with and those against them. We'll have to be cautious of all civilization while we set up a meet."

"Great," Manila said. "And here I was thinking we could have food and maybe a shower."

He shook his head. "Don't bet on it." Just then he checked his compass and smiled. "We're less than two miles out. You should smell the sea air pretty soon." He experimentally lifted his nose and thought he caught a faint tang. "Let's try to get as close to the coast as we can. We'll find a place to set up for the night and see if we can round up something to eat. Then we'll organize a pickup."

Everybody was now more energized, knowing that they were so close. As they stepped out again, this time Miles led the way. Manila fell into step just in front of Ryker and asked, "Do you think we can get help for Pablo in one of the towns?"

"I hope so," he said. "He won't survive the trip out of the jungle to his home, and all of us need rest too."

She sighed. "If we stumble across a town, there should be a medical center of some kind."

"That's the hope," he said. "Keep strong."

She shot him a smile and said, "Right." Just then came a noise up ahead. They raced to catch up to see they were at the top of a cliff, and the open shoreline sprawled in front of them. She gasped and said, "So beautiful."

"And so damn deadly," Ryker reminded her. "Now you really have to be on guard."

She shot him a look, and he nodded. "This scenario is more dangerous than ever."

CHAPTER 8

S HE STARED AT the signs of civilization down below. She wasn't even sure what town it was. It was a fairly good size and sprawled about, but they had to make their way down that cliff's edge, and they weren't even sure they could descend from here. She glanced over an exhausted Ryker. "Can we go down for the night?"

He studied the cliff. "I don't think we should chance it," he said quietly. "People are tired, and that's when accidents will happen. Plus, I don't see any place here to make our way down easily. Better we camp for the night up at the top and then try and find a way down tomorrow morning."

"What about Pablo?"

He nodded with a grim face. "I know," he said. "I want you to stay here with Miles, while I go check out a new location." Then he walked farther off the edge, where a lot of greenery could shield them from sight of anybody looking upward. But, at the same time, if the guerrillas were accustomed to this walkway path along the topmost edge, then their group would be in danger. He slowly lowered Pablo off his back until he rested on the ground. Pablo was mostly unconscious at this point.

Manila gently poured a bit of water on his head and tried to cool him. "He's burning up," she murmured.

"I know," Ryker said as he did stretches to ease his back

and shoulders. "I've got to see if I can find a way down." He walked over to speak with Miles for a few moments, and the two men talked as they stood at the top, looking down at the valley below. They weren't super high up, but it would be a hard jog down. Manila figured it may be a hundred and fifty yards straight down. The men pulled ropes from their packs, tying them together, while deciding where the best place to descend was. Then Ryker came back, and they hooked the rope's end onto a tree, and very quickly, he threw himself off the edge. She cried out softly.

Miles looked at her and said, "He'll be fine."

"Dear God," she said. "Surely there's another way to get down." She hated to feel the fear already sneaking through her at the idea of throwing herself off that cliff.

"Yes," Miles said. He came over and squatted beside Pablo to check his temperature. "Pablo needs a doctor."

"Well then, shouldn't he have taken him down with him?"

"He's got to see what the lay of the land is first," he said. "I might take Pablo down myself later, if Ryker locates a medical center or a hospital or something down there."

She nodded. "Right. I wonder if Ryker can casually do some grocery shopping while he's down there too," she said with a half a smile.

"Nobody can know we're here yet," Miles reminded her. "At least not until we know what the mood is regarding guerrillas down there."

"I know," she said, "but I could hope. I was looking forward to more of that fruit we had earlier, but I haven't seen any since then."

He nodded. "I know. I was looking for something to eat as well." He held out a bottle of water for her and said,

"Have a sip yourself, and then try to get a little bit down Pablo."

"He'll just choke," she murmured.

"He's not unconscious though," Miles said. He reached down and picked Pablo up a bit, so that he sat more upright. "Pablo, I want you to drink."

Pablo's eyes fluttered slightly and then closed again.

In a firm voice, Miles repeated, "Pablo, I want you to drink." He motioned to Manila to hold the bottle to his lips.

She gently held it to his lips and poured a little bit in his mouth. And, sure enough, Pablo swallowed. She managed to get what she would estimate was about a cup down his throat, and then Pablo refused more. She smiled and said, "Well, at least he got something down." She carefully wiped the edge of the bottle and then drank.

"It's not enough by any means," Miles said. "He needs medicine for the fever."

"I know," she said starkly. "So I guess it's down to whatever Ryker can find below."

"Exactly," he said. "It's not just about seeking medical help. We also have to set up a meet to get you guys out of here."

"I'd be totally okay to just go in town," Andy said. "Surely they're not against us."

"No," Miles said. "They're not. But they're also most likely for the guerrillas. What if somebody sees you and reports it to the guerrillas?"

"Why do they care?" Benjamin grumbled, as he came to a life a little more as he lay on the ground beside them. "My legs are like rubber. I couldn't possibly move if I tried."

Manila nodded with a soft smile. "Mine are too. But I can understand not wanting us going down that cliff in the shape we're in right now."

"But even in an hour," Benjamin said, "we'll have recovered enough to handle it. Food is down there. Beds are down there. We're part of a scientific trip. It's not like we wouldn't have considered arriving in a town like this any other time. Why do we have to worry now?"

"Maybe we don't," Andy said hopefully. "Once we're down there, we'll mingle in with whatever tourists there are."

"And you're assuming there are some," Miles said. "And maybe for you guys, it's all good. But I'm not sure that we're ready to take that chance."

"But you're acting like there's secrecy involved," Benjamin said. "We escaped the guerrillas. They won't come after us. They don't give a shit. We were in their space, and now we're not, and that's all they cared about."

"Yes, and no," Miles said. "You also escaped, and now several of their men are dead."

"Well, that wasn't us though," he said. "That was Ryker. We're not responsible for that."

"None of us are responsible," she said as she turned to face Benjamin. "It's not a case of being responsible but of defending ourselves. They were trying to kill us or take us captive again."

"Well, Ryker didn't have to kill them," he said.

"That's really not the point right now," she said, defending Ryker. "They were armed, going to shoot or kill Miles, trying to take us captive. We'd already been captive once. The last thing I want to do is be taken again. Besides, you've been more than happy to accept Ryker's and Miles's help all the way along the line. You can hardly just throw them to the wolves now."

"Stop being melodramatic," Benjamin said. "All I want

to do is go down to that town and get myself settled in for the night, where I can have a shower, a real bed and some food. We can arrange for Global to get us out of here in the morning."

"Do you think that's possible?" Andy asked. "Or is that foolish?"

"It's foolish," Miles said, sitting down and staring out at the coast in front of them. "Not only do we know nothing about what's down there, but do you guys have any of your personal gear?"

"No," Manila said, "but surely we could make phone calls somewhere in town."

"True," he said. "And maybe it's fine. Maybe the guerrillas and this town don't get along. Maybe they'll all see you as heroes because you survived."

"That's what I'm talking about," Benjamin said. He got up and walked over to the rope. "It can't be that hard to go down this rope. Obviously, our hands will get a bit chewed up, but we can bind them. I can go down there easy enough."

Miles looked at him steadily and said, "When you get down there, then what?"

"Then I'll find a hotel," he said stoutly. "I'll make a phone call, get a credit card that we can use—actually I already know my credit card number. I just don't have it with me—and I can get booked into the hotel. As soon as that happens, we're safe."

"What is it about a hotel and a night's lodging that you confirm as being safe?" Miles asked.

"What I don't want," Benjamin said, "is to consider this as some conspiracy theory. There's absolutely no need for secrecy now. You were supposed to get us back to safety." At that, he looked around and pulled off his T-shirt, ripping it and tying it around his hands. "I'll go down that rope. I don't want to even listen to you guys trying to stop me."

"Oh, but—" and he just glared at her.

"No buts," he said. "Nobody gives a shit about the guerrillas in the jungle. They live here all the time. This is a year-round situation for them. We ran into them, and that's it. I'll go and get a night's room and board." And he headed down the rope.

Manila winced as he managed to drop down the rope. "Do you think he's okay?" she asked Miles. "I can't imagine going over that edge."

Miles looked at her and frowned. "Are you scared of heights?"

"You don't have to be scared of heights to be scared about dropping yourself off that edge. I can't even imagine stopping myself."

"You wrap the rope around your leg," Andy said. "Most of us learned how to do that in the gym."

"I didn't," she said. "That terrifies me."

"We can still get you down," he said.

"Are you sure there isn't a walkway?"

"There will be," he said. "But we won't find anything like that until tomorrow morning."

By now, darkness had settled in. Andy got up and walked over to see what he could, and then he came back and said, "He's done very well. He's made his way to the bottom of the rope, and now he's walking to town."

Instantly, she stared up at him. "Damn. Now I want to go too."

"What about throwing yourself off that cliff?"

"Do you remember that part about how I can't imagine

that edge?"

"Of course not," Miles said. "But we can get you down. Don't worry about it."

"You don't think we should follow Benjamin?"

Miles shook his head. "No, I don't. At least not until Ryker returns."

She frowned and settled beside Pablo. "Regardless of what you and I think about us," she said, "Pablo needs attention."

He nodded. "And, as soon as we can, we'll get him there."

She didn't know how much time had passed. She collapsed under the cooler night air, watching the darkness blanket the village below as it lit up with some lights. It wasn't as big as any cities or towns, and she definitely saw no sign of Benjamin. She knew Andy desperately wanted to follow him down and have a decent meal himself, whereas she was much more concerned about Pablo. An odd whistle came in the darkness. Miles sat up and called out with a weird cry himself. She looked at him. "What was that?"

"That's Ryker coming back," he said.

She bolted to her feet. "Where?" She walked over to the rope to see Miles making his way along the edge and holding on to the rope. She glanced around, but Ryker came off the far side, and soon enough a male figure walked toward her. "Ryker?"

"Yes," he said. "I found the pathway once I got to the bottom."

She ran forward and threw herself into his arms. He held her close. She burrowed even deeper. "God, I was so terrified when you threw yourself off that edge," she whispered.

He held her even closer and whispered, "I've done it

many times."

Her arms clenched convulsively. "Maybe you have," she said, "but I haven't. That looked terrifying."

"Well, the good news is, there is a pathway. It's a bit of a hike and a climb, but it's doable."

"Tonight?"

"Only if you want to go over the rope first," he said. "If you don't, then we have to take the pathway, and that's not something to take in the darkness."

She thought about it and shrugged. "If I spend another night up here," she said, "whatever. Did you see Benjamin?"

He tilted her head up and frowned down at her. "Did he go down?"

"Yes, once he realized that you got down and that you were okay," she said. "He was adamant about going to the village and getting a hotel for the night."

"Interesting," he said. "Well, it's certainly possible he's fine. I found a medical center and several small hotels, so I'm sure he's in a room with a shower and a hot meal."

"Damn," she said. "In that case, I really, really, really want to throw myself off the edge."

"Most of the people appear to be fairly quiet down there," he said. "I didn't come across anybody aggressive, and certainly any guerrilla sympathizers won't be very widely public about their viewpoints. Whether the entire village is part of the guerrillas though, we don't know, but I doubt it." He walked over to Miles, and she joined him. But then he bent down and looked at Pablo and said, "We don't really have any choice. He's got to go down."

"That's the problem," she said.

He nodded and looked at Miles. "What do you think?"

"I'll take him," Miles said. "Tell me where we're going,

and I'll see if I can get some help for him." They quickly discussed it by diving in the map to see where the medical center was. Then they harnessed Pablo on Miles's back, and Ryker assisted him on the rope. She had no clue how they managed it so quickly, but he was quickly slung up and safe for the descent. "Interesting way to travel."

"It's easier this way when you're carrying a heavy weight," he said. And very quickly, Miles was off and down the rope.

Andy stood here and said, "As soon as he hits bottom, any chance I could go?"

"Absolutely," Ryker said. "Go." The rope suddenly relaxed as they realized that Miles had reached the bottom. Ryker leaned over the side, hanging onto the rope. He nodded and said, "Your turn." They used up the rest of Benjamin's shirt on Andy's hands, and he slowly went down hand over hand, carefully fitting the rope around his leg each time.

When he got to the bottom, he called out, "It's not that bad. Come on."

Ryker looked at her. She stared at the rope and swallowed hard and said, "I don't think I'm physically capable of going down like that, even before trekking twenty-two miles across a dense jungle."

He smiled. "You'd be surprised."

She nodded. "Well, I don't know how to stop myself from falling."

"You'll go after me, so I'm below you," he said. "And I'll take the weight if you slip, and we'll tether ourselves together."

"Seriously?"

"Seriously," he said. "If everybody else is down, we

might as well make the trip too. But only if you're comfortable with it."

She swallowed. "I'm surely not comfortable with it, but I really would like to be down there."

He quickly showed her how to work the rope around her leg and then lowered himself so that he hung there and said, "Now I want you to do exactly what I tell you."

And, following his instructions, she found herself suspended over the edge of the cliff. She took several deep breaths, trying to calm herself down. His voice was a steady guide as he said, "Now loosen it around your leg and come down one step again and again." And with him just barely below her, almost knowing that she needed that security of having him right there, she slowly lowered herself along the rope.

Halfway down, she could feel her arms fatiguing. "I'm slipping," she cried out, hugging the rope tightly and hating the fact that she was only halfway there. All of a sudden, he was there with her, his hands wrapped around her, holding the rope in front of her.

"We'll go together," he said. And slowly, with her arms resting on his, the two of them climbed down the rope the rest of the way. When she sagged onto the ground, finally at the end of the rope, she burst into tears. He wrapped his arms around her and held her tight. "I've never seen anybody do anything braver," he said.

She shook her head. "That wasn't brave at all," she said. "That was being a whiny and teary child. I couldn't have done that for the life of me without you."

"The thing is, you were terrified of it," he said, "but you did it anyway."

"But not without your help," she whined. "And halfway

down …" She was a little lost for words.

He smiled and tilted her head, then kissed her on the tip of her nose and said, "Now let's see if maybe we can get you into a little better scenario." They were almost at the village now. Andy had waited for them, once he realized they were coming, and the three of them walked toward the village. Ryker said, "I'm going ahead to the medical center to make sure that Pablo can get some care."

"Is there any law enforcement here?"

"There will be something," he said, "but remember. We're still foreigners."

"I know," she said.

Two hotels were before them. "I'll check which one Benjamin's in," Andy said. "I'll come back in a minute." Manila followed Ryker, knowing instinctively that he was her best bet to stay alive in this world gone crazy as he headed toward the medical center. She also didn't want to be separated for a lot of other reasons that she didn't want to examine too closely.

When Andy joined her a few minutes later, she asked, "Did Benjamin get a hotel room?"

"Yes, he did."

"Good," she said. "Do they have other rooms?"

"Yes. I've told the hotel manager that we're coming," he said. "And that there'll be four of us."

"Perfect. Let's get Pablo taken care of, and then we can return and maybe get a shower and a bed." Just the thought of it had her footsteps moving rapidly toward Ryker, who was just ahead of her. "I surely hope this is the end of the nightmare."

"Well, we made it to the coast, and we're in a town," Andy said, remarkably cheerfully. "I imagine that pain is seriously over with."

She smiled. "Now if only we had some of our own personal gear."

"We need to make some phone calls," he admitted, "but we should be okay."

Ryker stopped ahead of her, and he turned to look at them and asked, "Are you coming?" She raced ahead and then turned to look back at Andy. "If you want to grab a room, go on. We'll be there in a few minutes."

He hesitated, but she waved him off. "It just means you get in the shower before us because, when we get there, there won't be any water left," she said as a joke.

Andy smiled and said, "If you don't mind."

"Go," she said. "Just go."

Andy flashed a bright smile at her and headed off to the hotel. As she raced toward Ryker, he asked, "Did you want to go with him?"

"No," she said. "I want to stay with you."

"If you're sure," he said.

"Yes, I hired Pablo," she said. "I feel a need to see that he's okay."

"Got it," he said. "Come on then." They held hands and walked around the corner to the medical center. As they got there, Pablo was slowly lowered onto a stretcher. The doctor and a nurse were working on him right away. Miles looked up and smiled. "You got her down here."

"I'm sorry," she said. "I guess I haven't been very easy to deal with."

Miles looked at her in surprise and said, "You've been very easy to deal with. Don't ever think that. Let's just hope that we're in time to save Pablo."

She listened to the conversation with the doctor, and,

indeed, they definitely had some concerns about Pablo's condition as his fever was so severe. But he was in the doctor's hands right now.

She walked back to the door and asked, "Can we leave him here?"

"Yes," they said.

"We'll check on him in the morning." She smiled. "I hope he's okay."

As they stepped outside again, Ryker and Miles looked at her and said, "Are you heading to the hotel?"

She nodded. "Aren't you?"

The two men shrugged. "I'm not sure," Miles said. "We need a good night's rest, yes, but we have to check in with our contact first."

She nodded. "Let's get to the hotel and check in from there. There's nothing quite like a solid night's sleep. We need it tonight. Maybe you guys are used to being Superman all the time, but, for us, it's been a pretty rough day."

"You're right," Miles said as they walked toward the hotel. "Let's get a good night under our belt and then see what our next steps are."

"Do you think it'll still be a problem?"

"Yes," Ryker said. "I still think it'll be a problem."

"But why?" she asked softly. "You did your job. Look at where you got us to! I would never have thought this morning that there was any way we would make it to the shore or to a town by the end of the day."

"Maybe," he said. "But the thing is, just when you think that everything is good, we find out it's not quite so good. So, although I get that you want to drop your guard and think everything's okay again, still be cautious."

They walked into the hotel. The desk clerk looked tired

and harried. He frowned when he saw their clothing but dropped his gaze to the book and handed it to them to sign in.

"We don't have any money," Andy said. He stood here, waiting.

"I do," Manila said. She quickly walked forward and took one of the hotel's credit card slips, then wrote down all the details.

The hotel clerk looked at the number and said in a guttural broken English, "I'll have to call it in."

"You do that," she said. He disappeared in the office, while everybody signed the register. When he came back, he nodded and ran through the remaining vacant rooms. They had only two.

She nodded and said, "That's fine. We can double up."

He gave them rooms that had two beds and gave them the keys. As they headed up, Andy looked at her and said, "Who are you sharing with?"

Ryker stepped in and didn't allow anybody to argue with him when he said, "She's sharing with me."

"You're still that worried?" she asked, studying his features.

"Absolutely," he said. "I am still that worried."

Andy lowered his voice and said, "Seriously?"

Miles nodded. "We don't know what was going on up there in the jungle, so let's not be foolish at this point in time."

"Good enough," Andy said. "I don't care anyway. I just want a shower. It's too late for any food apparently. I asked. But we can get a good night's sleep and eat in the morning."

"Exactly."

They headed to their rooms, which were at the back of

the hotel and up one floor. The good thing was that the rooms were side by side. As Manila walked in, she smiled at the quaintness of it. This was a small town and not exactly your typical North American hotel, but it was a room with two beds, and, for that, she was damn grateful. She headed to the bathroom and cried out when she realized there was a shower. "Are you okay if I clean off first?"

"Ladies first," Ryker said, opening the patio door and stepping out on the small balcony.

"I won't argue," she said and closed the door. She stripped down as fast as she could and stepped under the first warm water she'd had in days.

RYKER COULDN'T QUITE dispel that sense of unease that had permeated him since they'd first seen the village. It should have been like they said, a good thing. They were here, and they should have been safe and sound, but it didn't feel that way. He didn't know if the guerrillas had a stranglehold on the village, but he knew that there had to be a lot of interaction with them. The guerrillas got supplies from somewhere, and business was business. There would also be a lot of relatives to all the guerrillas, those not involved in the war per se. Ryker didn't know the specifics here yet, but it was enough that it kept him on edge, wondering what was going on, what would happen next.

Knowing that she was in the shower and realizing just how long it had been since she'd had that kind of care, he walked to the beds and checked to make sure that they were the same size and then quickly pulled back the bedding on both so that she could go to sleep immediately when she came back out again. He himself had one of his bags and a backpack still on him.

Miles had been picking up the guns off the guerrillas, so they also had a ton of weapons, but they'd stashed most of those up on the cliff's edge with one of the bigger bags. They could carry down only so much weight on the ropes. They only needed so much down here. It would be easier to go up the pathway. In the morning, he'd grab everything and bring it back here. As a matter of fact, as he checked the time to realize it was almost midnight, he should probably plan on doing that before six in the morning. Walking around with that amount of firepower wasn't a good idea. He'd give himself six hours to sleep and then would head back out.

As he stood here in the cool evening air, the door beside him opened, and Miles stepped beside Ryker, and he quickly discussed the plan to return and get the gear in the morning.

"Good idea," Miles said. "Something's off. I can't figure it out."

"I know," Ryker said. "I'm not sure where the problem is, but something's wrong."

"We don't want to leave all the weapons up there either," Miles said. "What time do you want to go?"

"Six a.m.," he said. "We'll give ourselves a few hours of good sleep, and then one of us needs to go get the gear."

"I think both of us," Miles said, "but that would mean leaving these guys alone."

"Manila's team probably won't even wake up until eleven, if not twelve," Ryker said with a smile. "They're pretty exhausted."

"I know," Miles nodded. "I sent out a couple messages, when I first got in."

"Good," Ryker said. "I was just thinking about doing

that now. I haven't heard any response yet, but hopefully, somebody's on the way for our pickup."

"Now the question is, is it just us that they're picking up?"

"The company they work for, Global Mining Industries, should arrange for these guys to get out of the village, but I'm not sure what the fastest way is."

"They may have to take a vehicle all the way back to the nearest international airport or maybe some water trip."

"I know, but I'm still thinking that maybe we're all better off going out the same way."

"Depends. We can't just use Uncle Sam's generosity for no reason."

"Exactly. But I highly doubt that by noon tomorrow things will look anywhere near as amiable as they do right now," Ryker said, his voice harsh. "And I don't know if it's got to do with the men I had to take out today or the fact that the uncle had basically made arrangements for Pablo not to return home again. Or whether the uncle had arrangements with the guerrillas himself for the kidnapping of this group."

"When you think about it, some decent money is tied up with holding Global's geologist for ransom."

"I considered that," Ryker said with a nod. "In which case, I'm not even sure we've got six hours of sleep left." Just then he heard the water behind him shut off. "At least she didn't take all the water in the place."

"Andy's still in our shower," Miles said in an amused tone. "But he won't be long. He'll be sound asleep in no time."

"I wonder if Benjamin is okay."

"He'll be fine," Miles said. "He always is. It doesn't really matter what he does. He's one of those who looks after himself."

"I'm surprised he was out on a trip like this."

"Probably needs to be his last trip. Nothing like having something like this happen to reassess just what it is you really want to do in life."

"And how secure you want to live your life," Ryker added. "As for Manila, she handled herself well."

"I think Manila is more concerned about her rocks than anything. Although she's very worried about Pablo." He paused. "And, if things had gotten ugly in the guerrilla camp," he said, "her whole priorities would have shifted. As it is, we left her backpack of rocks up at the cliff top too."

Ryker chuckled at that. "I'll definitely have to pick those up."

"Absolutely," Miles said. "Let's hope that we can get it before anybody else does." Miles turned and walked back. "My turn for a shower. Check in with you at six." And he left the doors open to let a breeze flow through the bedroom. Ryker stood for a few more moments. He could hear the voices in the next room as Miles and Andy spoke. And that's when he heard something behind him. He turned to see Manila walking toward him. She had her underclothes on again and a towel wrapped around her.

"The shower is all yours," she said.

He nodded. "Just so you know, I'll be heading up that cliff to gather the rest of our gear first thing in the morning."

She sagged into the bed and shook her head. "I don't know how you do it," she said. "I thought I was fit and in good shape, and yet, today has finished me." She yawned and then stretched out on the bed, still with the towel wrapped around her.

"Take off the wet towel and just crash. I'll have a shower, and then I'll crash too."

She smiled and said, "Good to hear."

He walked into the bathroom and stripped off what he had left for clothing after he had used one of his layers for Pablo's bandages, and then stepped into the hot shower. He scrubbed down, taking off several layers of dirt, and, by the time he came back out to the bedroom, she was sound asleep. She had just the light sheet over her, and she was spread out like a little child on her stomach, but her legs and arms covered the entire single bed. He crashed down on his bed, atop the covers himself, with just his boxers on, trying to tell his mind to shut off and to stop working the angles. He wanted nothing more than to just slide over and spend the night with her. But they weren't at that stage yet. He wasn't even sure there would ever be an opportunity for them to get to that stage, but something was so damn special about her.

As he laid here, he heard an odd murmur. He looked over to see her head tossing and then turning, her relaxed body pose tightening up as her body curled in on itself defensively. She whispered and then murmured, only to cry out. She was caught up in a nightmare. He quickly hopped to her bed and wrapped his arms around her, then pulled her close, whispering, "It's all right now. Go to sleep."

She sighed, woke up slightly, and whispered, "Ryker?"

"Yes, it's me," he said. "Just rest and return to sleep. You're exhausted."

"I am," she said. "And every time I close my eyes, I see those damn guerrillas."

"Forget the guerrillas," he said. "They're nothing."

She gave half a laugh and smiled. "To you, they may be

nothing," she said. "But that was way too close an encounter for my liking."

"Maybe," he whispered, "but you're here now. You're in bed. You're safe now. Sleep."

She murmured and rolled over, then wrapped her arms around him and threw a leg over his and whispered, "Or we could enjoy having a bed together."

He sucked in his breath, his body instinctively reacting to her words.

She chuckled and pressed her pelvis tighter against his.

No way she couldn't feel his instinctive reaction, as her leg slid up over his hips higher and higher.

"I'll take that as a yes," she murmured and then latched her mouth tightly on his.

He shuddered as his body roared with heat, and he flipped over onto his back as she welcomed the opportunity.

Her body slid over his, and her hands and lips and fingers caressed and touched and stroked.

But he was already at the edge of his control, and the last thing he needed was more stimulus. But he couldn't move. It was such a novel, sensuous sensation. When he finally felt her hand sliding under the edge of his boxers, groping him gently, he shuddered. "Don't do that," he whispered. "It'll be all over before we have a chance to enjoy it."

"It'll be all over before we have a chance anyway," she murmured, "because I can't wait." And she lowered his boxers, and somehow she was without any clothing and positioned above him. With his shaft right at the heart of her, she slowly slid down until he was seated fully inside.

He twisted beneath her, his body pulsing with joy. He reached up to cup her breasts.

She pressed herself tightly against his hands, using his

arms for support as she started to ride.

His focus narrowed until it centered on just one thing right now, the only thing that mattered in his world.

Her.

CHAPTER 9

MANILA DIDN'T EVEN recognize her actions, didn't recognize who she was right now. ... Her body pulsed with need, and passion had taken over. She wanted this man like she had never wanted anything in her life. ... She rode hard, and she rode fast, and, when her body came apart, she couldn't hold back her cry. She collapsed on top of him.

He flipped until she was tucked up beneath him, driving deep inside, harder and harder. He leaned down and captured her lips, and she came apart for the second time, impaling her with his own passion and leaving her possessed in all ways. He shuddered hard above her. She moaned as he collapsed beside her.

He smiled and said, "I've never seen a more beautiful woman caught up in her passion as you were. You were—are—gorgeous as those sensations hummed inside me in the same way. Believe me. You can do that to me anytime."

A laugh escaped her, and she groaned. "My God. I'm so sore, and I'm so damn tired."

"Sleep," he said. "Just sleep." He rolled over and tucked her up, their bodies hot against each other.

She dropped her head on the pillow and whispered, "Don't leave without saying goodbye."

"We'll see," he said.

She took one deep breath and slowly let out the air.

He smiled and held her close, then waited until she dropped off. He took several deep and long breaths and fell asleep at her side soon afterward.

It was the sunshine and the heat that hit Manila first. When she slowly opened her eyes, she slammed them shut against the bright glare. She laid here, beyond comfortable, nestled underneath the sheets, her body sinking deep into the mattress. She was so damn comfortable and so clean and beautifully warm and, best of all, safe. She opened her eyes a little bit to stare beneath her lashes, seeing that the curtains were wide open, and the light shone in. A stunning view of the ocean was right outside.

She didn't even remember how much the room cost, and she didn't care. It was safety; it was security, and it was comforting at a point in time when she had been desperately in need. She rolled over ever-so-slightly, groaning at her aching body, even though it sunk into a featherlight mattress. It seemed like any movements hurt. The thought of standing up made her wince.

Yesterday had been one of the hardest and most grueling and painful days of her life. Actually, it was probably the worst. She couldn't even imagine all that they had gone through. It didn't help to think about it, but she couldn't stop dwelling on that. And when she remembered Pablo, that damn rope climb down the cliff, and even Ryker during the night, she smiled at that. The last thing she'd expected was to have hot sex with her rescuer.

She reached out an arm, but, of course, he wasn't here. He was probably up that damn rope, trying to get all their gear back down again. But, as her gaze wandered over the room, she saw bags and bags of gear and realized he'd already come and gone. She sighed, sat up slowly and moaned at the aches brought on by her movements.

A light knock came on her door. She pulled the sheet up to her bare chest and called out, "Who is it?"

"It's Ryker."

"Come in, of course," she said, tucking the sheet around her. She shuffled backward, wincing with every movement, until she leaned against the headboard.

He walked in with a tray carefully balanced in one hand and closed the door behind him. As he walked toward her, his gaze was quick and assessing.

She smiled up at him. "Outside of trying to move and feeling like somebody ran me over with a cement truck, I'm fine."

"You look divine," he admitted. "For what you've been through, you don't look like you've suffered at all."

"Well, looks are deceptive," she announced, "because that's crap. Just waking up and rolling over hurt."

He smiled at her. "Understandable. We covered a lot of miles yesterday."

She looked at the tray he brought. "Is that coffee?"

He chuckled and placed it on the small table by the window. "It so is. Do you want it in bed right here or outside?"

"How hot is it outside?" she asked. "I'm not sure I can take too much heat after yesterday." He opened the glass doors, and she could feel a heatwave coming toward her. "It's beautiful though," she admitted. She stared, undecided, when he pulled out a long awning and propped up stick stands for it to cover half of the balcony. She smiled in delight. "Okay, outside it is. At least we'll try it." Then she stood and groaned. "That means I have to put all those crappy clothes on again."

He stopped, looked at her, and said, "I took a liberty."

"A liberty?" she asked hazily. "You mean, outside of bringing me breakfast and coffee?"

He nodded and pulled out a small plastic bag from his pocket. He tossed it her way. It was rolled up into this tiny little ball. She looked at it in surprise and then pulled out a thin cotton sundress. "Oh, my goodness, it's gorgeous."

"Well, it's not perfect," he said. "But I figured that it had to be better than putting on your heavy dirty clothes again. Although you'll need them anyway later today."

"Right," she said. She quickly pulled the dress over her head and dropped it down. "I think it needs a bra though, doesn't it?" She did a slow twirl.

"Personally, I love the view," Ryker admitted. He was studying the plump stretched-out top of the sundress. "But maybe you should rinse out your nightclothes or your underclothes."

"Wow," she said. "I never even thought of that." She grabbed her underwear and bra, then headed to the sink and quickly washed them with soap. Then she rinsed them and said, "Where would they dry the fastest?"

"I think they'll be dry in thirty minutes anywhere here," he said with a chuckle. "At least right now. Once the humidity kicks in, it won't be so easy."

She hesitated and asked, "Do you mind? It seems rather intrusive to lay my underwear out on the deck."

He shook his head. "Honestly, I already did that with my T-shirt."

When she saw what he'd done, she shook her head. "My brain has not kicked in yet," she said. She laid her bra and underwear on the rail and then went back and filled the bathtub with a little bit of water and quickly rinsed and washed her pants and her T-shirt. She gave them both a heavy lather, ridding them of Pablo's blood and all kinds of unnamed dirt alongside the heavy sweat from her hike yesterday. Then she did the same with her socks. As soon as everything was clean, she wrung them out, and then walked out to the balcony. He held out his hand, surprising her. She gave him her pants and asked, "What's the matter?"

"Nothing," he said. "But I'm sure I can wring these out tighter than you." And he proceeded to wring the material so that water literally poured from it. She stared at it in shock. "I don't know how you did that," she said. "But if you don't mind …" She handed him her T-shirt and socks. Within minutes, they had all her clothing up around the railing and hanging off the awning. "They'll bake like crazy here," she said in delight. "Clean clothes!"

"I know," he said. "Now, your boots. Are they okay?"

She nodded but then said, "I'll grab my hat too. I'm sure it's more than sweaty." She did the same thing with her hat and looked around to see if anything else needed washing. When she realized that she was pretty well cleaned out of clothing otherwise, she put her backpack on the floor. It was filled with all her business stuff and rocks and her laptop. She felt better confirming they were there. Then she gathered the stuff that she had collected on the sink from her pockets and laid them on her night table. Then she walked outside again, still brushing her hair and smiling. "You have no idea how you taking a liberty has made my day."

He grinned at her. "Not every woman appreciates a man buying them clothes."

"Well, this woman really does," she said. "Particularly in these circumstances, so feel free to do it again."

"I found them by accident," he said. "When I was checking on Pablo, a little store was open, and they had these hanging up. They looked like one size would fit all, which took some of the guesswork out of my purchase."

"And yet, I'm sure your firsthand knowledge gave you exactly what my measurements are," she said cheekily.

"Well, it was the most excellent firsthand knowledge," he said, flashing her a wicked grin.

She felt the color wash up her cheeks, but she refused to be embarrassed. They'd had way too much fun, and she'd been way too exhausted. "I'm only sorry," she said, "that it was over so fast. But I was seriously tired."

"Well, depending on your plans, we might do something about that."

"And here I figured that we were leaving today," she said, cocking an eyebrow at him. "Aren't we?"

"Yes," he said. "Hopefully. But I haven't had confirmation of that yet."

"Well, now this is an idyllic holiday," she said, as she motioned at the small town around her. "I'd be more than happy to go for a walk."

He glanced down on her feet and asked, "Barefoot?"

She winced. "So maybe I'll send you out on an errand looking for a pair of sandals too then," she said with a laugh.

He just smiled and said, "Sit down, and let's enjoy the coffee."

She sat to find the coffee was thick and rich and darker than anything she'd ever had before. When she took her first sip, she stopped, paused and then let out a slow and deep breath. "Wow."

"Maybe you want some cream? I put it there on the side."

She carefully poured cream into her cup and then studied the pastries with interest. "Are these savory or sweet?"

"No idea," he said cheerfully. "I figured we could cut them all in half and try each one."

"Well, considering that I thought you had enough here for the whole team …"

"Hell no," he said, "but I need to eat too."

He picked up the knife and carefully cut the four pastries in half. They were all different kinds, and he grabbed the half closest to him. She immediately grabbed the other half of the one he had chosen. As she'd bit into the rich pastry, she moaned. "Oh, my God, there's nothing like real food after starving for a while."

"Right," he said. "Being in that tent with the guerrillas couldn't have been easy."

"No," she said. "It was hot. We got very little water and, of course, almost no food."

"Any idea why they kept you?"

"Not only do I not know why," she said, "but we also never did get any resolution to it. So I don't know if they're still looking for us."

"I think they are," he said. "As much as I hate to admit it, I'm fairly certain that there have been questions asked around town."

At that, her heart froze, and she stared at him in shock. "Please tell me that we're not in danger."

"I can't tell you that," he said, his tone serious. "There's absolutely no way to know just what's going on yet, but we will find out."

"If we could find the old guide," she said, "then possibly we'd get answers."

"But he's on the other side of the jungle," he said.

"I know. I wasn't expecting to be here at this point myself."

"Did you do any of your original trip in a vehicle?"

"Yes," she said. "We went inland as far as we could, and then we ended up on foot."

"Right," he said. "That makes sense."

"We also tried to get as many of the rock samples as we could locally on day trips, and I've already shipped those back."

"But these? How much do you plan to pick up and bring home?"

"That's what Andy was for."

"Lucky Andy," Ryker said with a laugh. "He's just an eager and strong back, isn't he?"

"He's a very talented university kid, looking for solid career experience," she said. "He was thrilled at the opportunity. Only after we were captured did he realize the negatives of the trip."

"And Benjamin? He seems like an odd person for the trip."

"I wanted to come alone, as you know," she admitted, watching his eyebrows shoot up to his hairline, "but Global would only let me come as part of a team."

"Well, thank heavens for that," he said.

"I don't know," she said, "because then we had to have two guides, and one of them ended up betraying us."

"All alone in the jungle would not have been a good idea either," he said.

"Benjamin was Global's choice."

"Interesting choice."

"As it is, we got into trouble with a team *and* the guides. And we would still be in grave trouble if you hadn't rescued us, so thank you. I think I completely forgot to mention that part yesterday, but I really do appreciate the efforts you went to."

"I don't mind," he said. "It's what I do."

She studied him as he looked at the platter of goodies again. "Do you really travel around the jungles and pick up kidnapped people?"

He looked at her and blinked, and his grin flashed again. "No," he said. "But I travel to hot spots with a small team—as in Miles and me or four of us sometimes. There's always trouble somewhere. If it isn't a kidnapping, it's often a murder for hire, and we're after the killers. It could be car bombings and arsonists too, and we're after the bomber or the firebug. It could be any number of things. And, on some occasions, it's all about a government, where government members have been taken hostage, and, even after a rescue, they need to have the government reestablished. But those require bigger teams and a whole lot of different scenarios. I'm doing smaller missions right now."

"None of it sounds like fun," she said quietly. With a shake of her head, she picked up a second piece of a treat and took a bite into it, almost melting herself as the buttery flavor exploded in her mouth and the sweet sugary goodness drifted down her throat. "As a matter of fact, it sounds like a terrible way to live."

"I used to be a Navy SEAL," he said. "And then I was asked to join a secret black-ops department. So it's basically the same thing but different."

"Don't you ever get tired of it?"

He looked at her for a long moment and said, "What do you say when people ask you, *Don't you get tired of looking at rocks?*"

"Of course not," she said passionately. "No two rocks are

alike." And then she realized what he meant, and she nodded. "So, just because you might get tired of some of it, you realize that there's a need and that this is what you do and that no two jobs are alike."

"Exactly," he said.

She glanced toward the bags at the front of the room. "I gather you had no problem going back up the hill?"

"Miles and I both went up," he said. "We were a little concerned that somebody might be up there, watching us, but we didn't see anybody."

"Was it dark out?"

"Doesn't seem it's very dark at all here," he said with a shake of his head. "We were back by thirty minutes past seven."

"And I was still asleep, I'm sure."

"Absolutely," he said cheerfully. "You looked delightful, but I restrained myself from crawling back in and joining you. I dropped the bags and headed out again."

With a happy laugh, heat flushing over her cheeks, she asked, "And that's when you went to get coffee?"

"No, I checked with Miles that Andy was doing okay, then we headed off to a spot where we could get communications up and running and contacted our bosses to figure out a plan to get you guys home."

"Well, there are such things as commercial flights," she said.

"No airport is nearby," he said. "So, short of taking all of you on a cross-country trip for many hours to get to the closest one, we're back to looking at waterways."

"Or a helicopter?"

"Our people have none close enough, so I asked at the police station. There isn't one here."

"Interesting."

He shrugged. "We aren't in a Western world as we'd like to think of it," he said. "And we're in a very isolated small village."

"I'm surprised," she said, adding to his comment, "that there was even a hotel."

"Two are here, but this looks like the cleanest and safest of them."

"Right," she said. "And, of course, I'm sure cash is king here."

"It is, but they did take your credit card last night."

"I wonder if they still will though," she murmured.

"Meaning?"

"If anybody finds out that we escaped the guerrillas, I wonder if they're guerrilla sympathizers and if they'll make life as difficult as possible or have already gotten out the word that we're here."

"Depends how much money the guerrillas lost with your escape. If they're not worried, as it's a minor loss to them, they'll chalk it up as the one who got away," he said. "Or, if they're looking at a much higher payout, then it's worth them coming back after you."

She could feel all the color washing away from her skin at that. "Do you really think that's an option?"

"I don't know," he said. "We're not sticking around much longer to find out."

She let out her pent-up breath slowly and nodded. "I appreciate that," she said. "I can't imagine the horror of getting into that same scenario again."

"There's also another problem," he said.

She winced. "I don't think I'll like this."

"It's quite possible that somebody in town might be

more than willing to hold you captive and tell the guerrillas you're here. Whether they join the guerrillas or not, everybody here has to live with them in one way or another."

"Don't the guerrillas live in the jungle and avoid the villages?"

"Of course they do, but everybody needs supplies at some time. Everybody needs a certain amount of medical supplies or treatment at some time too."

"Right. So their tents and their clothing and boots and military gear all have to come from somewhere."

"They can live off the land for a large part of their existence, but everybody has family and friends and knows somebody. A lot of these kids are ones who were kicked out of their birth family or ran away from home and had terrible home lives for whatever reason or ended up with no family and became orphans of the world, where it became second nature to join up with another kind of family where they're welcome."

"So, lonely misfits. Got it," she said with a nod.

"But you can't make a generalization of that," he said. "Hundreds of thousands of people have died in this war. Everybody—every one of the guerrillas—has lost somebody, and they know that, when they fight, it could be their last day."

"Okay. This is getting very depressing. But what does any of that have to do with me?"

"It might be that they think you know more than you actually do."

She stared at him in shock. "Say what?"

"Gold mining is very illegal here, but it's also very prolific and very profitable. I wouldn't be surprised if the guerrillas aren't involved with it themselves or haven't joined up with the drug trade and expanded into the gold trade. So what else is very valuable? Platinum. And what were you doing here? Looking for platinum."

"So they may want to have a talk with me about where the platinum is located?"

He nodded. "You just happened to fall into their lap, but they didn't get a chance to question you."

"No," she said. "But they left me with my backpack, so how does that work?"

"They left your backpack? They took the rest of your gear but left you that one?"

She nodded and pointed to the small bag on the side of the room. "It's got my laptop and a few other things inside."

Immediately he got up and walked to the bag and said, "I hadn't realized they had taken it away and then gave it back to you."

"Well, they did, and, because it was all rocks, I don't think they cared. Outside of my mini laptop, that is. But I didn't have my battery in my laptop either, so, if they tried to turn it on, it wouldn't have."

"Well, of course, they would care about a laptop," he said, frowning. "That makes no sense."

She stared at him, hating her sudden sinking feeling. "Do you think they're tracking us?"

"That would make them extremely advanced," he said slowly as he worked his way through the contents of her backpack. "But maybe not all that advanced." He pulled out a small handheld device.

"Well, that's not mine. What is that?"

"Something they can track you with," he said, leaning back and staring at it.

She groaned. "So, even right now, they know where we

are?"

He quickly took it apart and then grabbed the glass of water sitting on the tray. He dropped in a small black piece of it. "Well, they did," he said, "but now they don't. Not for sure. Except that we are still here."

"Doesn't there have to be a reason though for someone to track us? Why would the guerrillas bother? I'm sure that's not necessary. I'm not a big fish to them."

"No, but if the guerrillas are getting more business-oriented every day," he said, "it's quite possible that they are trying to stay mainstream or go mainstream. So letting you go without getting all the information that you might know was an opportunity that they didn't want to pass them by. So they could ask you later when they had further questions."

She shook her head. "But they were kids. Everyone older we saw were young adults, late teens even …"

His gaze was straight as he studied her face. "Adults will be behind all this. Someone's keeping it organized and running smoothly. Likely a big organization. And it'll be those men who are looking beyond what the guerrillas can do now."

"Particularly if they have met and paired up in any way with another massive organization, *like the drug trade*," she said, catching on all too quickly.

"Or the gold-mining trade," he said, nodding, "because most of what is mined is done illegally. I'm sure an awful lot of security is needed to keep the gold flowing. They'd be a perfect match for that."

"So pair up or the guerrillas are taking it?"

"Possibly." He paused. "My initial thought is that the guerrillas planted this tracker on you because you said they asked you about the gold mining in the area."

"Right." She shook her head. "I'm not searching for that here."

"So," Ryker continued, pointing at the tracker, "they could see if your actions confirmed your words. As long as you didn't stumble across a gold-mining operation, they might leave you alone."

"My God, that could have happened easily enough. We'd look guilty as hell and would be innocent nonetheless."

"Could be another geologic group."

"Right, but I'd think I hear of it, or Global would have, whether legal or illegal," she said, leaning back with a heavy sigh. "It really doesn't make it very easy to even mine in Colombia, does it?"

"Not with their current war-torn state. And not likely without an agreement with the guerrillas." He nodded. "But that doesn't mean that you're off the hook."

"So," she said, "the sooner we're out of here, the better."

"Absolutely."

Just then another knock was at the door. He got up and walked over, then tapped once slightly. Another tap came on the other end. He glanced at her and said, "It's Miles." She nodded and picked up her coffee, then waited for Miles to join them.

As Miles stepped out onto the small balcony with them, he smiled at her and said, "Don't you look a lot better."

"A lot better," she admitted as she stared down at her dress. "And this is, of course, thanks to Ryker."

"Makes sense to me," Miles said. "I did laundry myself, and I'm still wearing slightly wet clothing."

She noted he wore a black T-shirt and black jeans. "Won't the black attract the heat too?"

"But I can walk around town a little bit easier in these."

"And speaking of which," she said, her gaze going from one to the other, "how's Pablo?" She saw them both hesitate. "Tell me," she said. "What's the matter?"

RYKER WALKED TO the small table and pulled out a spare chair for Miles, then sat back down again. "Well, we'd like to think that Pablo is okay, but he wasn't at the hospital when I checked."

She leaned forward to stare at him in shock. He smiled and then grabbed her fingers and said, "Now that doesn't mean he's died, and it doesn't mean that the guerrillas came and stole him away either."

"What does it mean?"

"It means, after breakfast, we'll talk to a different group and see what happened to him," he said. "Nobody could tell us anything."

She sat back and pinched her lips together.

"Remember. He survived an awful lot already. I doubt he died overnight."

"He was in a really ugly shape," she said quietly. "I would not be surprised if he passed in the night."

"Well, let's hope not," Miles said. "We went to a lot of effort to keep him alive."

She nodded. "And I guess we can blame the guerrillas for that loss too, if that's the case."

"I'd say his uncle as much as anything," Ryker said. "I'd love to get the uncle's name and pass on the word as to what he did, but I don't think it'll do a bit of good in this place."

He watched as she turned to stare out at the ocean, the joy and the holiday spirit now gone as the reality of what they had survived settled in. She looked at Miles. "Is Andy okay?"

Miles nodded. "I just spoke to him. He'll join us soon."

She winced and looked around at her laundry. "Well, let me check and see if all this is dry." She hopped up, quickly checked and snatched up the few pieces hanging around.

"Leave the jeans until later," Ryker said.

She nodded and headed back inside to the bathroom to dress further.

Miles looked at him. "Got in deep pretty fast, didn't you?"

"I did," Ryker said. His tone was short and terse. "Don't read too much into it."

"Not reading anything into it," he said cheerfully. "But it doesn't mean that there won't be some repercussions."

"True," he said, "but I can't say I'm too interested in an ugly fallout."

"Doesn't have to be an ugly fallout," Miles said. "Depends on what you want."

"Is it wrong to say, *all of it?*"

"I don't know. *All of it* is asking for a bit much but, as long as you two are on the same page, then maybe not."

CHAPTER 10

MANILA CAME OUT of the bathroom with a few more pieces of clothing on, feeling better with her underwear and less conspicuous and vulnerable. It's not that she didn't trust both Miles and Ryker. It just felt more normal. As she sat back down again, Ryker poured her another coffee, and she took a sip, then shuddered and quickly added cream.

Miles chuckled. "It takes a bit of getting used to, doesn't it?"

She nodded. "That it does. So now what?"

"I'll check on Pablo again," Miles said.

She nodded. "He damn well better be there," she exclaimed. "That's just terrible if he isn't."

"No point in getting ahead of ourselves now," Ryker said. "I also need to send out some more messages and see what was lined up for our trip home."

"I was thinking it'd be nice to stay here," she said, "but you're making it sound like that's not happening."

"You have to consider that somebody here could be willing to send a message to the guerrillas that you're still around and maybe that you are more valuable than they had originally thought," Miles said. "Or that sympathizers here may have had some family in the guerrillas. So they may take our interactions with the guerrillas more personally. It's really hard to know."

"Right," she said. She stared at the beautiful vista. "It looks like such a beautiful holiday location, but really the same dark depths lurk below."

"Absolutely," he said. "We also don't know anything about what the guerrillas were after or why they were after you and how far they're willing to go."

"Well, there's that," she said, as she motioned at the water glass and the black spot in it. "Ryker found that in the backpack they allowed me to keep."

Ryker nodded and said, "I told him."

She wrinkled up her face. "Right. What about Andy and Benjamin?"

"When I brought the gear back—no trackers in any of that by the way—I did talk to Andy a little bit," Miles said. "He's feeling better."

She brightened. "That would be nice. He's a good kid. What about Benjamin though? Anybody checked in with him this morning?"

"Not me," Miles said.

Ryker shook his head. "Neither did I."

She sagged in her chair. "We should disturb him and wake him up in the process, as it's the only way to make sure he's even there."

"We'll assume he's there," Ryker said.

"Sure," she whispered, "but that's not necessarily the truth." She stared down at the food and asked, "Miles, did you want a piece?"

He nodded and grabbed one-half himself. Ryker grabbed another half piece too.

She put a half on her plate and watched as the men finished theirs off. "I need real food more than sugar," she said.

"Sugar is good for energy though," Miles said. "It's just that we burn through it very quickly."

"Right," she said. "I wouldn't mind walking around this little village. Maybe find a little restaurant." She gave them both a hopeful smile.

"And that part's not happening," Ryker said, his tone was firm. "We can't take the chance of anybody else here letting the guerrillas know of your presence."

Just then another knock came on the door. Miles hopped up and walked over to let Andy in.

As soon as Manila saw Andy, she jumped to her feet, ran forward and gave him a big hug.

He held her close and said, "Wow, I'm so glad that shit's over with."

She beamed up at him and motioned at the table. "Come join us."

He looked at the empty plate, and his face fell. "Like, I'm seriously empty," he said. "I need food."

"You can have the half on my plate, if you want," she said, motioning at the piece she had yet to start. He immediately snatched it up and ate it in two bites. "You are hungry," she said in surprise.

"I wasn't kidding when I said I'm empty," he admitted.

"Well, I'll head down and see about Pablo," Miles said with a wave.

"I sure hope he had a good night," Andy said.

"We don't even know where he is," Miles said. "When we were there earlier this morning, they couldn't tell us anything about him, other than he wasn't there at the hospital."

Andy stared at him in shock. "But where else would he be?"

"I don't know," Miles said. "I'm about to find out." He motioned at Ryker and said, "I'll bring food back too."

"I'll come with you right now," Ryker said. "Give me five, Andy. I'll load up on the coffee and some treats as it'll be at least an hour or longer before Miles get back." Then he turned to look at the two of them and said, "Do not leave this room. Do you hear me?"

She nodded slowly and said, "Take care."

"I'm going downstairs," he said. "I'll be back in ten."

He stepped out with Miles into the hallway.

"I didn't think they'd leave us alone," she said.

"Is it that bad?"

"There was a tracker in my backpack," she explained. "Maybe Alejandro put it in my bag, in case we got lost."

He stared at her in shock. "What?" Then he stopped, stared, as if processing, and then nodded. "That's a hell of a good idea."

"So, I don't know if the guides or the guerrillas were really bad at using it or if it was damaged somehow on the trip. Maybe it didn't like the humidity. I don't know," she said. "But the bottom line is, if it's working, anyone who knows it's there could know exactly where we are. That includes the guerrillas, since they went through our bags. However, they may not know what they were looking at."

Andy reached up a shaky hand and ran it through his still damp hair and whispered, "This is just too unbelievable."

"Let me tell you all their different theories," she said with a half laugh. And she ran through everything that Miles and Ryker had discussed so far. "But Ryker thinks the guerrillas left the tracker to see if we headed for any gold-mining camps. If so, they would have come after us."

When she ran dry, Andy stared at her in shock and said, "I want to go home."

"Me too," she said. "Me too."

Just then came a knock on the door. She hopped up, but Andy reached out a hand and said, "Let me."

She sank back down and nodded. "It'll be Ryker," she said. "It's probably time for him to be back with coffee." And she would cheerfully drink another pot. It was so good. Strong but good. She settled back to enjoy the view around her. But then she heard another male voice and turned to see Benjamin walking through the hotel room. She smiled up at him. "Wow, don't you look much better." But, in truth, he didn't.

He still looked edgy and pissed off. He slumped into the chair closest to her and said, "What the hell? How long have you been sitting here with coffee and treats?"

"Only for the last hour or so," she said cheerfully. "Andy just joined us too."

Benjamin stared at her. "I figured you'd probably crash and sleep all day away."

"Instead," she said, drilling him with her glare, "we got a hotel room last night, had hot showers and a good night's sleep. *Just like you*. And, so far, I've had coffee and a treat."

He continued staring at her, then looked at Andy, who held up his hands and said, "I haven't. I just got here. No coffee or treats for me yet."

Benjamin snorted. "But, of course, the guys are looking after her, aren't they? Just because she's a female."

"I don't think *just because I'm a girl*," she said. "But, if they are, I'm grateful. Sorry if I got coffee an hour ahead of you. But I didn't realize you were awake. I don't see you apologizing to us for getting a hotel room an hour ahead of us." She really didn't like his attitude.

"It's always that way," he growled. "Geologists get the fancy things, and we get the shitty leftovers. You guys always get better treatment and better pay."

"You could have gone to college and got a degree, just like I did. That was your choice and your loss. And, with you, the fact that I'm female to boot makes it all that much worse," she said with an eye roll. It's not as if she hadn't heard this many times before. It was always the same when guys like Benjamin were pissed about the fact that her wages were more than theirs. But they hadn't done the university work she had done, and, of course, it was back to that age-old experience versus education. Not to mention blatant sexism. She was at the point now though that she had the university education *and* the experience, so it should have stopped a lot of the BS whining and complaining. Only it never seemed to. "Did you see anybody when you came in last night at all?"

He shook his head. "I was so tired. I got my room, came in, stripped off and collapsed on the bed. I only had a shower this morning. I couldn't have managed anything last night."

"I didn't think I'd sleep unless I was clean," she said. "I was so damn hot and sticky."

"Maybe," he said. "I'm feeling better now. And I did manage to make a couple calls last night."

"To Global?" she asked in surprise.

He nodded. "Took three attempts to get one call through, but I did let them know where we are and that we needed a way out of here."

"Good," she said. "I'm glad they know."

"What did Global say about the guerrillas?" Andy asked.

He shrugged. "I didn't give them too much of a play-by-play about it. Just that we were taken prisoner and rescued, and now we're in a village looking for a way to get home," he said. Then he glared at her. "I also used your credit card."

She raised an eyebrow. "I didn't know you knew the number."

"I always memorize the numbers," he said with a shrug. "We need something like that for a place like this."

"I thought they would only take cash myself," she said.

"They called and confirmed my number. That's the only reason they took it."

"Right. So, in other words, you paid twice for the room just because of the fact that that's how much they would charge."

He shrugged. "I honestly didn't give a damn last night. And, right now, the fact that there's food, and you've already had some pisses me right off."

And again someone knocked on the door. It was more like a boot kick though. Manila froze and then realized it was likely Ryker. But Andy was already up and heading toward the door. She watched, hating to be anxious, but after all the things that could have gone wrong this morning, the last thing she wanted was anything to disrupt the mostly idyllic scene—notwithstanding Benjamin—they had going on now. Thankfully it was Ryker.

His eyebrows raised when he saw Benjamin. "Good morning, sleepyhead," he said.

Benjamin glared at him.

Ryker ignored his attitude and placed the tray down, then handed out cups. Thankfully there was enough for Benjamin too. Ryker quickly poured the coffee and cut the treats. But this time, there wasn't any sharing. Benjamin reached and grabbed. She settled back with her coffee and studied the three different men. All were at different stages of life, and some were happier than others with where they found themselves. She would happily travel with two of them again, but she hoped to never have to do another trip with Benjamin. He was just way too sour for her liking.

As the atmosphere lightened, and the people had relaxed a bit more with food in them, she could feel her own tension dropping. Then she turned to Ryker. "Did you get through?"

"I got a couple messages through," he said. "We'll hear back in two hours."

"Hear back about what?" Benjamin asked almost belligerently.

Ryker looked at him. "For a way out."

"Right," he said. "We could always rent a truck and drive to the airport."

"That's probably … what? Six to eight or maybe ten hours away?" Andy asked.

"Doesn't mean there are any international flights either," Manila said. "So we'd be flying to the nearest city and then out."

"I don't really care," Benjamin said. "As long as we're on the move."

"That's the plan," she said. She looked at Ryker. "There's another issue that I never thought to bring up. Andy was taking pictures of the guerrillas. I don't know if that may have something to do with why they're still after us though."

Instantly, silence fell on the table.

Andy muttered, "Shit."

She shrugged. "Sorry. I didn't know if there was any reason why that would be a problem. I figured that, if we brought it up, Ryker would know."

"May I see the photos?" Ryker asked.

Andy got up in an instant. "I'll get my camera from my room."

He disappeared, and Ryker looked at Manila. "When did you find this out?"

"I knew all along, but I only thought of it now. He kept his camera on him a bunch, but he always kept it out of sight. It's expensive, small, easy to carry around, and the guerrillas may not have known what it was."

"It's dangerous to take pictures of them like that," Ryker said.

"Right," she said gently. "But honestly, I'm not sure that the guerrillas even knew."

"Right."

Just then Andy returned. He handed over the camera, and Ryker immediately went through the gallery of photos. "Lots of faces," he said, yet he connected the camera to his phone via a USB cable, already downloading them and sending them off to Mavericks central command.

Andy shrugged. "Faces interest me. They tell of an entire world in a small expanse of skin."

Benjamin snorted. "That's such a dopey thing to say," he said.

Andy glared at him.

"I think it's great," Manila said. "Andy, at least, was thinking about other things than himself."

Benjamin stared at her. "What the hell does that mean?"

She gave a heavy sigh and snapped, "Forget it."

Benjamin subsided, but he didn't look happy with her. But then, what else was new?

WITH BENJAMIN AND Andy right beside her, Ryker excused himself for a few moments and stepped out in the hallway. He quickly answered Miles's call. "What's up?"

"Pablo is here," he said. "But he's in a room in the back of the clinic."

"Did they tell you that he was there?"

"No," he said. "But I've just cornered a young doctor who admitted that they moved Pablo out of the public eye and into a back room after hearing his story."

"Pablo told them?"

"Yes."

"So they've moved him for his own protection?"

"It appears so. The village generally has a peaceable relationship with the guerrillas, but the members do come down and try to coax young men and women to join them. Pablo's at the right age for that."

"But he's not likely to join given what they did to him," Ryker said. His voice was hard as he remembered the slices on the young man's body.

"When I say *coax*, I mean *forcibly convince*," Miles said.

"Right. In other words, he wouldn't have a choice, and, if he's injured, then he *really* wouldn't have a chance to fight them off. Plus, if they're still after Manila, then that's even more of an option to grab Pablo and to force him to tell them where she is and then either take him into the fold or dump him off somewhere where he'll get eaten."

"Exactly," Miles said. "He's recovering though. He's on antibiotics, but he needs a few days in the hospital. He's quite worried. He doesn't have money, and he doesn't know how to get home."

"Something else that we didn't really consider," Ryker said. "We were just trying to keep him alive. But I don't think he's safe to go home. Not with his uncle."

"I'll talk to Pablo again in a few minutes," he said. "I just wanted to give you a heads-up that he's here."

"And find out if he has any idea what the guerrillas' plans were and whether they're likely to leave Manila alone or not."

"Will do," he said. "I still think regardless that we need to get her out of this place and back home again, so keep trying to see what you can come up with."

"I'm on it," he said. He walked down to the hall that had a window staring out over the expanse. And then he heard whispering off the side. He turned to see two of the hotel employees, both men, speaking in low voices, but they were gesturing toward the room that Manila was in. He stepped forward and immediately approached them. "What do you know about that woman?" he asked in a harsh voice.

Both men immediately clammed up, their expressions turning sullen.

"If you think to bring her any more grief," Ryker said, shoving his face forward, "you'll have to deal with me. Do you understand?"

Both men glared at him.

"You're working for the guerrillas, aren't you?"

Both men's eyes widened, and they immediately shook their heads.

"Yeah, you are," Ryker said in disgust. "I wonder how the rest of this town will feel about that. Are they all on your side? Are they all guerrilla sympathizers?"

"No, you can't do that," said one young man. "We'll lose our jobs."

"Oh, so you care more about your jobs than the life of that poor woman. She already escaped them once. Why do they care?"

"I don't know that they do care," he said. "They just put out the word to see if anybody knew where she was staying."

"So they come into town, do they?"

The same man nodded. "They do. But not in a large group. Just one or two. They have sources here and also get some of their supplies here."

"They probably do for every village though. They have a network of spies of which I believe you two belong to."

The men shook their heads. "No, but they pay money sometimes," the man said. "They just want information."

He looked at the second man who, so far, hadn't said a word. "And what information will you give them?"

He gave an innocent look and said, "None."

"Meaning, you've already passed on that information, haven't you?"

Instantly, the younger man stiffened. "I didn't say that," he snapped.

"You don't have to," Ryker said. "I can see it's written all over you. When did you tell them and when can I expect to have visitors?"

The young man looked at his buddy and asked, "Did you already talk to them?"

He shot him a hard look. "You don't get paid for nothing."

"Sure, but we also can't just turn her over to them."

"Why not?" he said sullenly. "They're nothing but foreigners. We don't need their kind here."

"Idiot. You must have tourists at this hotel to have your job here. And yet, if you give her to them, she'll be here a hell of a lot longer," Ryker said. "So I'm not leaving here until I find out exactly what you said and when that'll happen now that you've told them." There was silence in an instant. He checked his watch and said, "You've got no idea who you're dealing with, so feel free to take a seat because you'll be here for the next couple days, in with the town's doctor, … or you can talk now."

"You can't hold us here," the young man said.

"And why is that?" Ryker asked with interest. "The guerrillas held her and her team for a whole day. I mean, what do you care, right? We'll just retaliate and show you the same treatment she got. In which case, of course, you don't get food or water, and we'll march you into the jungle and leave you to suffer the heat and the snakes the same as the guerrillas did to her."

The young man shook his head. "They're not like that," he said.

Ryker snorted. "Seriously, is that what you think? Do you realize one of her guides was sliced up and dumped for the animals to feast on, alive?"

At that, the young man paled. "I didn't think they did things like that."

"They are guerrillas," Ryker said. "They like to think they are soldiers. All they give a shit about is fighting."

"They're fighting for a cause," the second man cried out with heavy emotion.

"Absolutely," Ryker said. "And we don't know anything about that. But what we don't want to do is get involved again. So why would you tell them where she is?"

"Maybe because they don't want her lost in the jungle," the second man said, his voice turning crafty.

Ryker gave him a flat stare. "You can tell your guerrillas that she leaves today under our care, and, if they want to bring on a war, then bring it here to the village."

"You can't do that," the younger man said. "Innocent people will get hurt."

"And who do you think she is?" Ryker asked, his eyebrows going up. "She's a geologist here, looking at rocks. She's innocent in any part of whatever hellish nightmare scenario you guys were told."

"But that's not true," he said. "She's dangerous. She's spying for the government."

Ryker snorted. "Have you seen her? She's not a spy, for your government or for hers. She's not anybody other than a geologist fascinated by rocks. She works for a US company, and they sent her here to look for platinum."

The young man looked confused. He glanced at the second man, but he wasn't having anything to do with it.

"Right," Ryker said. "Well, let me call for my backup. We'll take you into the jungle. We'll tie you up and see how long you last."

"Wait, wait, wait," the young man said. "You can't do that."

"I can do anything I need to do to keep her and her team safe," Ryker said, his voice low and intense. "And, as you seem to think that it's totally okay to sign her up to get kidnapped again and to get tossed into the jungle and tortured and God-only-knows-what-else they'll do to her because she picked up a rock that she was legally allowed to do by your own government, then you've got another think coming."

Footsteps echoed by the stairs. Ryker turned to see the owner of the hotel coming in.

The owner immediately asked, "Is there a problem?"

"Depends if you're a guerrilla sympathizer or not," Ryker said, his voice still low and steady.

The hotel owner's face twisted with scorn. "They took my son, and they ruined my daughter," he said. "They can keep their war to themselves in the jungle."

Ryker motioned at the two men standing here. "Well, these two men just sold the guerrillas information about the people who I came with here," he said. "And I'm getting pretty angry myself."

"As far as I'm concerned, they can return to the jungle and be tied up and deposited for the guerrillas. They're always looking for new men. They can have these two new converts." The owner glared at them.

At that, both men jumped up and said, "No, no, no, we're not joining them."

"Yes, you are," Ryker said. "I'll tie you up with a big gift-wrapped bow and dump you in their camp if it's the last thing I do." He meant every damn word of it. "For trying to send those three innocent people—that woman in particular—back into their clutches, I'll make sure that the guerrillas know you're willing but just need to have your minds changed."

Both men immediately paled and shook their heads. One man said, "I have a wife and a baby."

"Oh, that's good," Ryker said. "They'll want your wife too."

At that, the young man turned all shades of color, and he said, "Look. We didn't mean any harm."

"You already accepted money, and, if you did it this time, you've done it many times," he snapped.

At that, the hotel owner reamed them out, his Spanish fluid and with a dialect that Ryker couldn't even begin to understand. But the tone was easily understood. The owner was not only disgusted but he was also angry that they, as hotel employees, would use their access to the hotel guests for such purposes. Both men followed an order from him and pulled out the money from their pockets.

"Is that all she's worth? That's the extent of what a woman's life is worth? So show the guerrillas where your wife is—and is that all I would get for her?"

"No, please, no," the young man cried out in fear.

"Why shouldn't I? It's not like you care about women—this one in particular—do you?" Ryker snapped, driving home his point.

Both men looked ashamed. "It's hard to make money here," the younger man said.

"That's not an excuse," Ryker said. "She's a person and not just a victim here. You have no business making her life a living hell." He turned to the hotel owner and said, "What will you do with these two?"

He was still obviously angry. "If I fire them, these two worms will just return to the guerrillas and tell them what's going on here. They'll come and burn down my place," he said in disgust. He turned and spat at the men's feet. "I'll be speaking to my manager about you two."

They both backed up, and Ryker said, "You two need to quit giving information to the guerrillas, accepting money from them, don't you?"

Sullen, the two of them looked at him and said, "You didn't have to tell him."

"I wouldn't have to if you two were being cooperative," Ryker said, his voice low. "And believe me. At this point in time, if I find out anybody else is coming here, we'll use you on the front line." He turned to the owner and said, "And that's not a bad idea. I want both men standing guard on our rooms."

The owner looked at him. "Why would you want that?"

"Because then, when the guerrillas come," Ryker said, "I'll throw these two to the wolves."

"You can't do that," the young man cried out yet again.

"And why can't I?" Ryker asked. "I'll give them the two people they were looking for, except that you'll take their places."

"That's wrong," he said. "We didn't do anything."

"Seriously? You just sold a woman to the guerrillas."

CHAPTER 11

Restless, Manila didn't know how long it would take for Ryker to come back. She'd finished the coffee, and the two men were arguing over what their next step was, when Benjamin hopped to his feet and said, "Okay, I've had enough of this place. I'll tour the village." Then he looked at her. "Somehow you ended up with fashionable clothes, but you're still barefoot."

She looked down at her bare feet and nodded. "The only thing I have to wear is my boots," she said. Then she motioned at his getup. "You have your clothes from yesterday, and I still do too, but then I'd have to get changed."

"No point," he said. "You'll slow me down. Besides I don't want to be seen and I can do that better without you." And he walked out.

Andy said, "He doesn't mean it that way."

"Yes, he does," she said. "I've never seen that totally sexist side of him until this trip."

"Have you done trips with him before?"

"No," she said, "not really. Not long ones like this."

"I think it really grates on him that you make more money than he does."

"And that's always the balancing act," she said. "I don't know if it's because I have a degree, and he doesn't, or because I'm female, and he thinks I get special treatment for that."

"And yet, the truth of the matter is, most times it's the men who get a higher paycheck. So that's probably a large part of it."

"Benjamin's the kind of guy who'll complain no matter what," she said. "If you want to go with him, then go. I'll sit here and relax. My body needs to recover from yesterday." He hesitated, but she waved him off. "Go on and enjoy."

He smiled and said, "Ryker said he was outside, so you should be okay."

"I'm more than okay," she said. "I'll probably take another nap." She pushed her chair back and checked her jeans on top of the awning. Then smiled and said, "At least I have clean clothes."

He looked at them and smiled. "That was very smart."

She nodded. "Go on. Enjoy your afternoon."

"Wait. Wasn't Miles supposed to bring food?"

She nodded. "He should have been back by now, I thought." Andy hesitated, and she said, "You can always check back and see if the guys are back with food while you're out. The first flush is over now that you've got some treats in you, so either go for a walk and come back, or, if you see Miles or Ryker, you can always come back with one of them."

He flashed her bright smile. "I'll do that." And he walked to the door.

She was amazed at the resilience of youth because, in truth, she was flagging again, seriously and badly. With her clothes folded and sitting on the edge of the bed, she climbed back up on top and stretched out, then dropped her head on the pillow. She didn't know where Andy got so much energy. She was dead tired. But then yesterday had been brutal in so many ways. She wished Ryker would come back soon.

He'd said he'd step out for a few moments but whatever was going on sounded pretty off to her. But she'd had so much coffee that she should have been running around in circles, and yet, instead she yawned like crazy. Surely a little nap wouldn't hurt. She wasn't even sure what time it was, but it had to be close to noon. She let her body sink once again into the fluffy bed. She was quite content to stay right now. As much as she'd like to be a tourist and walk around, the footwear was an issue, and, if a tour meant getting back into her heavy clothing again and lacing up those hard boots, she was totally okay to stay barefoot. Besides she was supposed to stay out of sight, and that would be impossible.

As she thought maybe she could drift off to sleep, she heard a light knock, and the door opened.

"Going to bed?" Ryker asked.

She smiled without opening her eyes. "The guys left, so I was thinking I would relax a bit more. The thought of getting dressed again and putting on my heavy work boots was more than I could contemplate."

"Are your feet sore?"

"A little bit," she said.

Just then, gentle fingers picked up her feet and gently checked them out.

"You've got pretty big blisters," he said. "That's not good."

"I was trying to ignore them," she said. "We trekked a lot of miles in rough terrain."

"I know, but you'll have to put those boots back on again when we leave."

"I know," she said. "I don't even have bandages."

"I'll fix that," he said. "Back in a minute."

He walked over to his bags. She watched as he went into a small pack and returned, then lightly covered her blisters with ointment and then with bandages. One of the blisters had opened, and, even as he put a second bandage on top, the second blister popped. "That'll help them to heal too," he said as he quickly cleaned them and rebandaged them.

"Now my feet don't look anywhere near so nice," she said with a laugh.

"They look beautiful, like the rest of you," he said. Then he glanced at the table full of cups and plates. "I should clean that up too."

"I can help," she said, swinging her legs over to the side and sitting up. "I didn't want to waste an opportunity to lie down and relax."

"Just stay there," he said, waving her back. "I'll put everything back on a tray and put the tray outside the door." And, with that done, he took it out and laid it on the floor to the side of the door.

As the door opened, she thought she saw somebody standing there. "Who's out there?" she asked. He hesitated, and she shook her head. "No more secrets, please. What's going on?"

And he told her about the two men who work for the hotel.

She paled and stared up at him, firming her lips even as her stomach churned. "They really were doing that to me?"

He nodded. "You have to remember that they weren't necessarily doing it to you. You weren't a person. You weren't a woman they knew or cared about. It's not as if they would do it to their own families."

"In other words, I'm just part of a profit-making

scheme," she said.

He nodded and shrugged. "It's humanity at the worst of times, unfortunately."

She nodded. "Isn't that the truth? But it sucks."

"It does," he said. "But they'll stand there on guard."

"Just means that they'll let anybody in."

"But we won't be here," he whispered. She looked at him in surprise. He walked out onto the balcony, and, before she realized what was going on, he motioned for her to come. She walked outside, and she saw two boards crossing the balconies to Miles's balcony. She stared at it and shuddered. "Are you serious?"

"Very serious," he said. "I want you to crawl from here to there."

He helped her up to the side, and, with Miles at the other end, and her refusing to look down, she slowly crawled and made her way across the balcony. When Miles lifted her off, she gave him a big hug and said, "I really don't want to do that again."

"I understand," he said. "And, if we didn't have to, it'd be much easier." And just then, he hopped up onto the two boards and met Ryker, who was on the other side. Ryker handed him off bags and bags of stuff.

Then, with everything moved over to Miles's room, she asked, "But what about Andy?"

"Hopefully we won't have to stay here," Miles said. "At least not for very long. But, if need be, Andy and I can stay in your room tonight."

"Is that fair though? What if the guerrillas come in after me there?"

"Hopefully it's not even an issue," he said. "We do have to get out of here in a fairly reasonable time frame today."

"And what about Pablo?" she asked.

"Well, I have good news for you there."

She stepped inside Miles's room, realizing it was pretty well a duplicate of hers and sat down on the bed. "Tell me," she demanded. "Is he okay?"

He explained what had happened and why he'd been given a private room off to the side to keep him safe. Her face lit up. "So, not everybody in this village is like those two assholes outside my room?"

He shook his head. "No, and most people don't deal with the guerrillas at all. They keep quiet. They like to ignore the fact that the guerrillas even exist. I also questioned Pablo as to the guerrilla's plans and if you are likely to be in any danger still, but he didn't have an answer for me."

"So potentially safe except for those guys standing guard?"

"Yes, and oddly enough," Ryker said, "one of them is married and with a young child."

She frowned. "And he was prepared to throw away another woman like his wife?"

"More a case of another woman so that his wife could have a better life," he corrected.

Her shoulders sagged as she realized just how much of an opportunity that would be here. Most of the people would be happy with the simpler life but you would always get the young men who weren't. "I'm still not terribly impressed," she announced.

"Neither are we," Ryker said. "And, by the way, you said that the men went out. Where did they go?"

"Benjamin wanted to go for a walk around the village, and Andy was interested in finding food or crossing paths with Miles," she said. "Nothing is wrong with that, is there?"

"No, hopefully, they're not gone very long," Ryker said. "We haven't gotten our orders confirmed yet, but chances are, when we do, we'll have to move fast."

She looked at Miles. "Did you bring food?"

He smiled and nodded. Then he walked over to the desk at the front of the room and motioned at the two large bags.

"Right," she said. "So, can we sit outside and have it there?"

"Well, to hide that you're here in this room now, I suggest we eat inside," Ryker said.

She nodded. "That's reasonable. We could also move to another place entirely."

"Only if you know where we can go," he said.

"It's already past two, so I have to pay for a second night here anyway," she said, sagging back on Miles's bed. "Did you remember to bring my clothes over?" she asked Ryker.

He nodded. "I did." He motioned to the folded stack of clothing on the side, and she smiled.

"I just hated to leave my clean clothes over there. Did my boots come too?" She turned and looked around.

He frowned and said, "No, I guess not." He walked back out and without even putting the boards back up, he quickly made his way over to the other side.

"How did he do that?" Manila asked.

Miles laughed. "Well, I could say he's half monkey, but the truth of the matter is, we were trained to do this stuff all the time."

She sighed. "Maybe, but it's still pretty amazing."

"It is. It's almost magical," he said with a laugh. Then Ryker appeared again, walking through the balcony door with her boots.

"Now, whenever you leave our rooms though, you

should be leaving from that door, shouldn't you?"

"Now that the two men are on guard, yes," he said. "I'll stage it to look like you're alone."

She swallowed hard. "Are you expecting one of them to do something?"

"I am," he said. "It would be nice to put a stop to this."

"What about Pablo? Is he safe in this town?"

"I'm not sure," he said.

"More concerning is how to get him back to his family," Manila said.

"Does he even want to return?" Ryker asked. "His uncle gave him to the guerrillas and ditched him in the jungle, and he quite likely paid that guide to do it too."

"Maybe he can find a life here then," she said. "He was looking for work, and there wasn't any at his home."

"Well, maybe the hotel has a spot now," Miles said. "Especially with those two losing their jobs."

"It's possible. It's hard to say though. I'm afraid that'll be Pablo's cross to bear." Ryker shook his head. "I don't know. I'm sure there are multiple ways to travel around here, but it might take him a week if he's determined to get home again."

"I feel like we should help him," she said. "We're responsible for him ending up here in the first place."

"Yeah," Miles said. "We're responsible for him still being alive." He winked at her, and she laughed.

"I get that, but, at the same time, it sucks."

"Not to worry. We'll make sure that he's not just dumped here."

"Any idea if we can leave today?"

"I don't know yet," Ryker said. "It's already two-thirty. I would hope so, but I can't say for sure."

"I want to relax and enjoy being here, but, at the same time, now I feel like I can't do that."

"Until you're back home again," Miles said, his tone very serious, "I highly suggest you don't relax at all."

"Right," she said. "And that's terrible. It's life, isn't it?"

"It so is."

She groaned. "So, food?"

The men quickly rearranged some of the furniture, so they could sit around the small table in front of the open glass balcony doors. And then Ryker brought over a selection of what looked like meat and vegetables and lots of rice.

"This looks wonderful," she said, as she scooped up some for herself onto one of the plates that he had brought over and then served them each a serving as well. "Did you intend this for everybody, as in all five of us?"

"More or less," Ryker said. "If we need more, we'll get more. What I want to do is make sure that your tank's topped up just in case we have to go for a long time without again."

Her fork froze in midair as she contemplated that. When he gave her a steady look and nodded, she sighed and took the bite anyway. "I really don't want to have to do that anymore."

"We're not safe yet," Ryker said. "Remember that. Don't let your guard down."

"Fine," she said. "I'll eat, and then I'll have a nap. Because, while I'm stuck in here, I might as well at least regain some energy too." And she quickly polished off her food, then got up and grabbed the top blanket and laid down on top of Miles's bed. She pulled the blanket over her shoulders and slept.

"THAT WAS FAST," Miles said. "She ate and then fell right asleep."

"At least she's using her reserves for what's needed," Ryker said.

"Are you really expecting the guerrillas to come today?"

"I don't think it'll be the guerrillas at all," he said. "I think it'll be somebody who's a sympathizer and informant for the guerrillas."

"More than those two guys?"

"I think they were paid pennies," he said. "I think somebody else in town here is likely running messages and doing whatever the guerrillas need."

"Maybe, but it's not like the guerrillas have money."

"Except now that they have partnered up with the drug trade, that's not quite true. They have way more money than we think."

"So what are you're expecting to find?"

"I'm not expecting to find anything," he said. "I just want to make sure that we're out of here before anybody else tries anything." Just then, his phone beeped. He checked the messages coming through and said, "That's Asher. Looks like a naval ship's not too far away."

"We'll get there how?"

"Arranging for a Zodiac," he said. "We'll meet at the beach at midnight tonight."

"That works," Miles said. "That's really good timing. If she can sleep now and then eat again, we can get her to the beach and get out of here before things go to hell."

They heard an odd sound outside. "I think that's already in progress," Ryker whispered. With a hard look at Miles, he rose and walked to the door, but Miles followed him and said, "Remember? It's my room." He stepped out and heard some heated voices outside. Miles spoke calmly and said, "I'm sorry. I don't know where they are. I think they're sleeping." A couple more voices spoke, and then a man stormed off. Miles stepped back in. "So, that looked like the hotel manager talking to the two young men again."

"Right," Ryker said. "If we're certain that those two snitches are sympathizers, chances are the manager is involved with the guerrillas. Otherwise, why would these two men be following orders like this? Still, the owner seemed to take a hard line against the guerrillas, so I wonder where the manager stands on the issue."

"Right, and it would make sense that he would see and know people around the village. So then we have to get out of here now?"

"No," Ryker said. "We'll stay as long as we can. And just when they think that we're settled in for the night, and the manager's planning whatever he's planning, he'll find out that the room next door is empty."

"I like it," Miles said. "I think I'll head back down to the hospital and talk to Pablo again. See what he can come up with for his plans and any other guerrilla contacts around here. And maybe speak with that young doctor."

"I'll come with you," Ryker said. Then he frowned at the bed where Manila laid. "But I'm not sure if we should leave her alone."

"Stay," Miles said. "I'll be back in a few minutes."

"You mean in an hour." Ryker checked his watch. "It's almost three o'clock, and, with any luck, she'll sleep until four."

"I'll be back around four or five then," he said. "If Andy

or Benjamin return, give them some food and try to get them to stay here, just in case we have to pull out earlier."

"Will do."

At that, Miles stepped out. He spoke to the two young men outside Manila's door too, his voice carrying easily, and then he headed down the stairs. Ryker very quietly locked the door and headed back to the table that he quickly cleared off. Then he pulled out his laptop and brought up the chat window and told Asher where they were and what was going on. He wrote, **Don't know what's happening with the hotel owner, but the hotel manager could be a sympathizer with the guerrillas.**

We can't get you out before midnight, the chat message came back. **So make sure you stay safe until then. The photos you sent of local guerrillas didn't get any pops. No one showing up on our Most Wanted lists, including Interpol. The guerrillas won't win any brownie points by taking you out now. With any luck, if we make it too difficult, they'll give up.**

I highly suspect that's the answer, Ryker typed, **but I've got two young men standing watch over her room now.**

And that's not a bad idea. If nothing else, they'll tell the guerrillas that they were forced to do this, and that she's in there.

That's what I figured, he said. **It's still dicey but get us out fast.**

Got a question for you, Asher texted.

What's up?

How well do you trust her team?

I don't trust anybody, Ryker said. **What about them?**

Benjamin's in financial difficulty, Asher said. **As in grave financial difficulty. He's losing his house. Do you**

think he'd have something to do with the guerrillas?

Yep, without a doubt. He's slime. Ryker sat back and thought about it. **What happens if she doesn't return?**

Well, he's next in line for the promotion at Global.

But he doesn't have a degree.

Which is why she got the job in the first place, Asher said. **Doesn't mean that he wasn't eligible. Apparently, it was a tough decision.**

So then will he likely get offered the job if she doesn't return?

Unfortunately, that's quite a big possibility, he said. **An ugly one but definitely a possibility. Still not a huge motive for murder.**

For Benjamin, it is. He can't climb the career ladder on his skills alone. So what about Andy? Any problems pop for him?

No, Asher said. **Unfortunately, he's new. He's just a student who's trying hard to make his mark in the world and to grow his career.**

Agreed, Ryker said.

At that, Asher signed off and left Ryker studying the coastline and their rendezvous spot. He didn't trust anyone. Silence was the best option. And, therefore, he wouldn't tell Andy or Benjamin what they were doing until it was time to leave.

"Anything wrong?" Manila asked.

"No," he said, turning his head and smiling at Manila, who laid on the bed, cozy and sleepy. "Return to sleep."

"How long have I been out?"

"Only about ten minutes," he said, although it was probably closer to twenty minutes. She yawned, and he said, "Just sleep. The best thing you can do now is sleep."

"Sounds good," she muttered. And she quickly closed

her eyes and fell asleep again.

With her quietly snoring beside him, he went back to researching which of the naval ships would be closest and how long it would take to reach them. Out in the ocean on a Zodiac, they could be up against all kinds of weather. A small boat would get buffeted badly. It would be all about fuel. And that was a concern. They had to make sure they had enough to get where they needed to go.

He quickly mapped out the best landing spot and sent them to Asher and then looked at the time frame to get back from one side to the other and realized that the reason it would be midnight was because it would take that long just to get the Zodiac to them. Too bad no helicopters were around. They could just land the damn thing beside the town. But that was way too easy. And it certainly wouldn't work in this instance. Not within their optimum timing. But he thought he'd ask. **No helicopters close by?**

Nothing that will do the distance. The destroyer is coming toward you as it is. So, with any luck, your trip won't be too long.

We're still talking four to five hours before the Zodiac reaches us?

Five hours going against the current, yes, Asher said. **And five hours is doable.**

As long as it comes with a ton of fuel, Ryker said.

Yes, it will. Once you're out in the ocean, everybody'll be looking for you—those on our side, that is. So don't worry about it. We got this.

I know. It's not me I'm worried about. It's the passengers.

Are they okay?

Yes, he said. **But it's been a rough trip.**

Manila is apparently pretty tough though, Asher said,

so I wouldn't worry about it.

So, if I told you to not worry about Mickey, would you have listened to me?

There was silence and then he came back with a **Hell no.**

Exactly, Ryker said. **And that's how I feel about this one.**

Interesting. Glad to hear you found somebody.

I'd be glad too, if we were out from under this scenario, he said. **But I can't guarantee that right now.**

Of course not, but you're a good man, and you will look after your own.

Sure. It's just doesn't necessarily correlate to mean that she'll be safe.

You've only got a few more hours to go, Asher said with a smiley emoji. **What could possibly go wrong in that time?**

Ryker groaned. **Don't even say that.**

I know, Asher said. **That's like a death sentence and asking for everything to go wrong.**

Absolutely, Ryker said. **And what we really need is for something to go right for a change.**

Well, you're not in the jungle. You're in a hotel, and you're safe and sound for the moment. That's an awful lot of *right* to me.

Okay, I'll give you that. But, in the meantime, I need eight hours just to get our ship close enough to us, he said. **And then another four or five hours with us in the middle of the night on a Zodiac in the ocean.**

And, for you, that's easy-peasy, Asher said. **Good luck.**

And Ryker signed off.

CHAPTER 12

MANILA WOKE UP from her nap, feeling groggy and disoriented. But then she finally recognized that she was in a different room. Although identical, it wasn't the same. At least not a hundred percent. For one, it didn't feel like home, and the bed that she had slept in last night had that added extra something to it. But then maybe that was because she had also been with Ryker. Now she felt like a visitor again. She stretched as she got up, doing a couple floor-to-ceiling stretches to ease the aches and pains in her body. And then realized she was all alone.

Her team had headed into town, and Ryker should be around here somewhere. She didn't remember what he was doing. She stepped out onto the balcony and studied the distance between the two balconies, then shook her head. She still didn't believe she'd crossed that. But then, after what she'd been through, it was just one more thing.

She ducked back inside, not wanting to stand outside too long, and brought her laptop out quickly and used it, connecting to the Wi-Fi network. Thankfully they had that here. Immediately, she got on with the university and talked to several of her colleagues. Global had emailed her several times, and she opened up a conversation with them.

They had heard about her from Benjamin, confirming what he said he'd done, and that they were worried about how to get her home again. Conversations flowed back and forth, and she said that she thought she had an answer, but she was waiting on the team who'd rescued her to confirm it. There was absolutely nothing else she could do but wait. She did have samples and had found a couple good prospects, but the conditions here were pretty rough, and they would be up against guerrillas on a constant basis, so maybe they should look at other countries with better mining opportunities.

A noncommittal answer came back after that, and she just shrugged. It wasn't her problem. They'd either make good with the government and the guerrillas, or they'd end up with a fight. Again, it wasn't her problem. One of the questions that came back was how did Benjamin and Andy hold up. She replied that both were fine. They were both different in their own ways, yet she wouldn't blackball either of them.

Even Benjamin?

She stared at that question for a long moment. **He obviously wasn't pleased with what went on, but yes. Why?**

He's registered a complaint against you.

She stared at that in shock. **About what?**

The fact that he believes you were at fault that you were captured.

At fault? She asked, anger rising up within. **I was following instructions, collecting from the best data points that we had established prior to leaving. The guerrillas came upon us early in the morning. We were fully surrounded before we ever left camp. The camp location was decided based on the guide's recommendation.**

There was no answer for a long moment. **Noted. We'll discuss it with him when he comes back.**

And me. I need to be part of that discussion. Sounds like he's holding a personal grudge. And I have seen some of that here in his attitude.

In what way?

Apparently, he knows or assumes that I make more money than him, and he has made several jabs about that during the trip, including me being a female, and I think he's more or less done with this entire process.

No longer a team player?

She thought about it and shrugged it off. I'm not trying to diss him here. It's been a rough trip for all of us. But the sooner we all get back into our normal surroundings, I hope some of the hard feelings will settle down.

Yet he's made his complaint official.

Good to know, she said and refused to go down that path. What is the process for me to refute it?

We'll have a sit-down meeting when you get back.

I presume that choice was between which of the two of us would take the lead on this job?

No, never, her boss said. Your job position originally was between the two of you. You were hired since you've been there, and we're more than happy with your performance over the last several years. He would never be the one to take this trip as a lead.

It could be that it's time for him to consider retiring or taking another type of job in life, she said. His job dissatisfaction is fairly obvious. But then again, we've been under a tremendous amount of strain. There's nothing like being taken prisoner to have you reevaluate your job choice. She ended that with a laugh, sending a smiley emoji.

You stay safe, and let us know when you come in.

Will do, she said. Then she quickly ended the chat and

closed down everything, including her laptop. It was incredibly small and, even in its case, fit into a particular pocket on her backpack, which was, as far as she's concerned, the only reason why the kidnappers hadn't taken it. The fact that it was surrounded by rocks may have helped too. They had been pretty disgusted when they'd seen her rocks, but the guerrillas had left her with them. Then again it was to their benefit as well to have the rocks come up as containing platinum. Because, if anybody could find something like that in their part of the world and mine it, then they could certainly step in and mine it themselves, just as they were doing with the country's gold. Although it wasn't the guerrillas doing the mining, she couldn't help but think that all these industries were working with each other and against the government. She didn't really blame them. It wasn't exactly a Western society they all lived in.

She quickly packed up the rest of her stuff so that she had one bag and her clothes to get changed into were at the foot of her bed. Then, not for the first time, she twirled around in her dress, loving the way that the skirt flew open. It was just such a hot day and such a lovely gift and very thoughtful of Ryker. She checked her watch and realized it was late afternoon already, and somebody should be here by now.

She hated waiting. She didn't have any way to contact any of them without her phone though. As far as she understood, nobody had phones. Not her team anyway. That was something the kidnappers *had* recognized and had taken. Not to mention a lot of their survey gear and anything they recognized as valuable. So they had left her the rocks.

She looked outside into the late afternoon sun and realized it was too hot even here at her balcony door. So she stepped farther inside. She'd eaten, and she'd had coffee, but now it felt like she was alone in the village. She dared not leave without shoes on her feet, and she didn't really want to get changed yet, although she would within a few hours. But if she had a few hours without her hot outdoor gear on, then she'd appreciate it.

She wanted to head out and take a look around but couldn't, considering she was under strict instructions to stay here. She understood that, but it seemed like she was missing out on an opportunity that everybody else was enjoying, and she wasn't. It sucked. She walked over to the hotel room door and would have opened it but then remembered the fact that those two men standing guard at her hotel room door had sold her to the guerrillas, and nobody was to know that she was here instead.

She raised her hands in frustration and threw herself on the bed. Just then she heard an odd noise. She slowly straightened and stared at the front door, but she wasn't sure that the noise had come from the door as much as it might have come from the room beside her. She tiptoed across the room and held her ear against the wall to see if she could hear anything.

Definitely somebody moved around in there. But that could just as easily have been Ryker, making sure they'd emptied everything from the room, or even Miles determining that they would stay there for the night. But that hadn't been the plan. The plan had been that they were leaving tonight, and, if anybody was coming and going into that room, then Miles and Ryker would go across the balconies, not enter the front door—not without exiting that front door first.

She shook her head and muttered, "Something weird is

going on." *Someone's on the other side.* But it could easily have been one of the two men who had supposedly been standing guard too. Frowning, she wanted to go out onto the balcony but that too would reveal where she actually was. Then she heard voices. And somebody saying that they had to find her. At that, her heart froze. She raced to the glass balcony doors and quickly closed, then locked them and checked her hotel room door. It was already locked.

Just then, the door quickly opened and shut really fast. She spun around to see Ryker. She raced toward him and threw herself into his arms. "*Shh*," he whispered. "It's okay."

She shook her head and pointed at the room beside her.

He nodded and placed a finger against her lips. "I know."

She stared up at him. "What's going on?"

"I don't know," he said, "but we need to get you out of here."

"How?"

He glanced at her dress and lack of footwear and frowned.

"I can get changed," she said.

He checked his watch. "You might as well anyway."

She snatched up her clothes, went into the bathroom and quickly pulled on her slightly stiff jeans. She also wore her T-shirt, and, when she came back out, she put on her socks and then stuck her poor feet into her boots. She walked experimentally around, hating the blisters but knowing she had no other option.

"How are your feet?" he whispered.

She shrugged. "They're not bad. I'll survive as long as we're not doing another thirty-mile hike."

"Not today," he said.

She nodded and bent down on one knee, then tightened up her boot so that they were as good as they could be for walking around securely. And then she took the dress and folded it gently and rolled it up as tight as she could. She tucked it into one of the side pockets of her backpack. And that's all there was left of her things. She lifted her bag, winced at the weight of the rocks, and said, "Are we clearing out?"

"We'll take anything you feel you need to take, just in case," he said. "And we'll come back and get the rest of it later."

"Do we need anything though?" She glanced down at one long duffel bag he had, which was full of weapons, and then his own bag.

"No, not necessarily," he said. "But I'm not sure that we want to take everything right now."

"Well then, we can leave it here, and we can go for a walk around the village," she announced. "As long as I'm with you, they'll think twice about coming after me."

"Well, we can check out a rendezvous spot for tonight."

"Let's go." Immediately she held out her hand. "As long as you think it's safe."

HE STEPPED OUT first, noting that the two guards weren't at their post. He quickly sent Miles a note, updating him on that event. He swept her down the hallway to the back stairs. Just as they were going around the corner, he could hear men's grumbling voices and stomping. He rushed her forward and whispered, "That's the guards."

He caught a glimpse of them coming up with platters of

food before they retook their spot in front of her door. He grinned at that. But it also meant that whoever else had been in her room had known Manila was not there. He immediately suspected either the manager or the owner of the hotel.

And the only thing he could think of was some sort of agreement with the guerrillas. And he didn't know that they operated on that level. It was too damn confusing, and he didn't really care about getting the final details as long as he could get her out of here.

Outside, he watched as the humid and hot air hit Manila's face full-on. She took several deep breaths and said, "Wow, so hot and humid. It was much cooler in the hotel room."

"We had the air-conditioning on," he said.

She shrugged. "But I was outside earlier."

"With the door open," he reminded her.

She nodded and hooked her hand through the crook of his elbow. "Can we stop and see Pablo too?"

He considered the suggestion, then nodded. "That works. We'll go there first." He led the way to the hospital, and, as they stepped in, the doctor looked up and frowned.

"Pablo's not here. I told your friend that already." His broken English came out testy, as if he was tired of being nagged over something.

"He's not here at all?" Ryker asked in confusion.

"Where could he be then?" Manila asked.

The doctor stared from one to the other. "I don't know. He checked himself out."

"Was he in good-enough shape?" she asked in surprise.

"Somewhat, yes," he said. "The antibiotics kicked in, and his fever broke. I don't know for how long he'll be okay. Depends if he rests up somewhat."

"Good," she said, showing her relief.

"Maybe," Ryker said, but he could feel her fingers gripping his elbow tightly.

"He was doing okay though?" she asked persistently.

The doctor nodded. "We gave him several doses of heavy antibiotics and cleaned out his lacerations. He obviously needs to rest, but he was doing much better. We also had him on IVs for hydration, and he's fine now. Or will be fine," the doctor corrected.

"And he checked himself out?" Ryker asked.

The doctor nodded again. "That's what I said. Now can you guys stop bothering us, please?"

"Well, since this is the first time I've been here," Manila said, her voice stiff, "I wanted to confirm for myself that he's okay."

"Then track him down," the doctor said. And he turned and walked away.

The receptionist gave them a half smile. "We aren't used to people coming and going all the time."

"Of course you are," Manila said. "You're a hospital. Everybody comes to visit, looking after their loved ones."

"Yes, but this guy came in last night. We put him into a small separate room, so he could stay away from everything and everyone," she said. "And then, as soon as he could, he got up and left. I think that's what the doctor objects to mostly. He feels like Pablo's a fugitive, and he's helped him."

"He helped him stay alive," Manila objected. "That's what a doctor does." But she spun on her heel. "Come on."

Ryker nodded and smiled his thanks to the receptionist and asked, "Did he pay for his care?"

The nurse winced and shook her head. "That's probably what the doctor's more worried about."

Ryker pulled out several American hundred-dollar bills and placed them on the counter. "I know it's not enough, but we appreciate it."

The nurse took it in, surprised. "No, but this will go a long way to helping that," she said. "Thank you."

And he quickly stepped out with Manila.

She stared up at him. "I didn't even think of that."

"No such thing as a medical plan here," he said. "Somebody has to pay for his care."

"Right, and we did look after him, so it does feel like we should be looking after him more."

"He's the one who's checked himself out," he said.

"Was he really afraid the rest of the villagers would know he was here?"

"I think they were trying to keep him safe, and he was just trying to stay safe. The guerrillas went to a lot of lengths to make sure he didn't survive."

"And is that even fair? I don't understand that."

"I don't either," he said. "Come on. Let's head down to the beach."

They walked in silence most of the way. He studied her face often, loving to see her turn her full face against the breeze and just inhale the salty seawater scent. "You really love it out here, don't you?"

"I've always loved the outdoors," she said. "And, of course, look at the field I went into."

"And is that a field where you would expect to always be outside, doing trips like this?"

"Over the next three to five years, I would expect to," she said. "As you move up in the company, you can stay home more often. But it's hard to say." She shrugged. "I'm not quite ready to give up the trips yet."

"Good," he said. "As long as you're enjoying yourself, then you shouldn't have to."

They kept walking along the edge of the beach as he studied the coastline.

"How long a trip is it tonight?"

"Depends on how far in the ship can come," he said. "But we're looking at about four to five hours at a minimum, just to get us from the shore to the ship. Could be several hours longer."

"Rendezvous at midnight, so maybe, if we're lucky boarding, it'll be by early morning? Like a normal early morning, I mean. Like, six a.m.?"

"Something like that," he said.

"You sure it isn't easier to just fly out?"

"Fly from where?" he asked. "No airport is anywhere close to this village. We could bring in a float plane. But, given the weather forecast, that might not be a good answer. We could drive to the next city, but I don't know if I want to try that."

"Why?"

"The guerrillas are everywhere," he said quietly. "I don't know if they're more pissed off that you escaped or pissed off that you were a potential gold mine for them."

"Likely both," she said sadly. "I didn't really get any feeling that they cared about who we were as much as what we could do for them."

"Welcome to life in Colombia," he said.

She nodded. "Still sucks."

"I'm still wondering if anyone else knew about the tracker in your bag," he said.

"I don't know." She smiled and shrugged. "And it wasn't much of a tracker, was it?"

"No, but it did the job," he said. "It let them know we arrived at the village."

"True," she said, frowning. "And it should have told them where we were in the jungle."

"Yes, but the jungle is not that easy to track for signals. So it depends on who was receiving the tracker data. If they weren't the guerrilla part of the search party, then they wouldn't have had any way to know exactly where we were. If it was just Alejandro with a handheld transmitter and receiver, then likely, it was for his use to keep you safe."

"True enough. Okay, so we'll just leave that one for the moment," she said. "Say it was Alejandro who gave it to me. He may have explained at the time, but I honestly didn't pay him much attention. More that it was yet another safety rule to follow. I was telling Benjamin about it earlier. But it could also be that others knew it was there too. Like the guerrillas. Particularly if it's common for guides to use in this area."

He looked at her, frowned and said, "I wonder. Did Alejandro appear to be that sophisticated?"

She shrugged. "I don't know. I don't know what the norm is on something like this. But if the guides can't afford to lose their people, maybe it makes sense so they can always find out where they are."

"Maybe," he said. Inside, he wondered about such technology. "The old guy, was he friendly?"

"Very," she said.

"I wish I could return to where you were actually taken from so I could better study the tracks and see who and what happened."

"I didn't get much of a chance to do or see anything," she said. "I was out with Andy, collecting rocks, and Benjamin was with the two guides."

"How far away were you?"

"About a mile."

"You didn't have a guide with you?"

"We were going back for a third trip, and I was the one insistent about that trip," she said.

"And, when you got back to camp, what did you see?"

"I didn't get a chance to see anything. It was early morning. I went into my tent, and, when I came out, we were completely surrounded already. There was Andy and the young guide and a half-dozen armed guerrillas. We were marched through the forest until we came up to the camp where they kept us at."

"And did you ever see the older guide again?"

She frowned, and he watched as that quick intelligence of hers whispered through the possibilities. Instead of looking for the answer to his question, she was looking to understand why he'd even asked it. "I'm not sure that I did," she said. "Maybe he heard them come and disappeared."

"Maybe," he said. "How close was Benjamin to your camp?"

"Well, he was supposed to be halfway," she said, "but he was at the guerrilla camp when we got there. So I don't know if he just was rounded up earlier or if he left his position."

"Was he within sight of you at all times leading up to your capture?"

"He was supposed to be," she admitted. "But I stepped around the corner, looking for another vein in the rocks."

"That's the only time he was out of sight?"

"Until Andy and I decided we were coming back, and we couldn't see him then. But we didn't really worry about it because we weren't looking for trouble."

"And he should have been with a guide, right?"

"In theory, yes. One should have been with him and one at camp."

"And they were supposed to stay close all day, correct?"

"One was to be with us at all times, yes. But we've been working together for days already, so they already knew my habits, and I don't think that was at the top of their list of things to worry about."

"Maybe not," he said, "but it's hard to say."

"What difference does it make?" she asked. "It was just a bad scenario. We were completely surrounded and taken prisoner."

"But nobody saw the old guide."

She shook her head. "No," she admitted. "I didn't."

"And who put the idea in your head that he was the one who had brought the guerrillas in on this?"

"I don't think I heard anything about it until we found the injured younger guide," she said. "But I don't remember. I just figured he got smart and managed to escape and took off."

"And forgot about you?"

"If you think about it," she said, "any guide would."

"Not all guides," he said, "but maybe some of the guides would have gone back to get help."

That stopped her in her tracks. "In which case, they would have gone back to where we were and that would put them in more danger."

"Maybe," he said quietly. "And it's also quite possible that he got killed in the fray."

"And yet, he was the one with all the experience," she said. "At least, according to Pablo."

"How did they treat each other?"

"An easy camaraderie, although they obviously had their issues," she said instantly. "I don't think they were buddies, the way they talked back and forth."

"Then what was the relationship, do you think?"

"More like teacher and student. The older guy was the more senior one and was showing Pablo the ropes. Pablo, more or less, did what he was told to do. They were joking about a knife that Pablo really liked, which was the older guide's."

"Alejandro?"

"Yes," she said. "The knife was from his grandfather. Pablo really liked it. But Alejandro wouldn't let him use it."

"And was it a friendly conversation?"

"Yes, it just became something that they argued about every day."

"Whatever," he said, dismissing it. But, in the back of his mind, he wondered.

"I don't understand this line of questioning," she said. "What's it all about?"

"Maybe nothing," he said. "It's a little confusing what's happening here."

"True," she said. "I wish we had seen Pablo though. I really want to know that he's okay."

"True. Did he have a phone at all?"

She looked at him in surprise; then she shrugged. "I don't know. I didn't see him with one, but that doesn't mean anything. The guerrillas took ours away."

"No," he said. "It really doesn't. But whatever, we'll see." He pointed just then to an outcropping of rocks. "That's a possible place."

"Sounds like we'll get soaked," she said.

"Maybe," he admitted. "But it won't kill us if we do."

"Can't we get onto it from the shore?"

He pointed at the huge rocks. "It's likely a Zodiac—a Navy SEAL boat. It's not the best to bring in on rocks like this."

"But they must handle a certain amount of rough terrain."

"Yes, but we're also looking for a location to reach in the dark." His gaze swept along the coastline, looking for a better landing spot.

Then he came around the corner on another beach, and he stopped and looked at the cliff around them. "Let's climb up over here." Thankful that she had her boots on, she followed his lead, and they made their way up to a small ledge that overlooked the area. And down below were several boats tied up and several others farther out fishing.

"Is there a problem?" she asked.

He studied the area and shrugged. "No, I don't think so."

"Where's Miles?" she asked.

He slid her a sideways glance. "I haven't heard from him in a little bit," he said. "He was going to check on Pablo."

"Only Pablo has left," she said. "For that matter, both Andy and Benjamin have left too. Speaking of which …" She told Ryker about the conversation she had with Global.

He looked at her in surprise. "Benjamin has filed a formal complaint about you?"

She shoved her hands in her jeans and stared out at the water. "And I'm really struggling with that too. There wasn't any bad blood between us before this trip. Not that I knew of anyway. But now … Now it feels like everything's wrong."

"Some trips and some days can be like that," he said.

"It's almost like it's a reset once you get home. Or overnight even, if you're lucky. You have a good night's sleep, and you wake up the next day, and everything's changed again."

"Maybe," she said. "But I doubt it will happen in this instance."

"I know," he said. "Something has been wrong right from the beginning."

As they turned to look around, she said, "We're not very far off from the spot where we were originally, are we?"

"We're a whole lot lower," he said, motioning up to another cliff. "We were up there. I didn't realize that we had this lower ledge here. It would have been much easier to rappel down from here."

"Well, at least I had my one experience jumping off the cliff."

He laughed and said, "You did really well."

"No, I didn't. I blubbered like a baby the whole way."

"We're all forced to the edge of our endurance sometimes," he said. "It's how you step up and show who you really are at those times of stress which makes all the difference. You didn't back away. You faced the challenge, and you survived. That's what counts." He looked down at her and dropped a kiss on her forehead. "Come on. We can walk to the water now too."

And, just then, a shot rang out. She cried out in his arms and collapsed.

CHAPTER 13

S HE OPENED HER eyes, hearing an odd whimper, only to realize it came from her throat.

"Hush," he whispered as he carried her rapidly down the cliff edge.

"What happened?" she murmured. He jolted suddenly, and she cried out yet again.

"If you can, hush," he said. "I don't want to have to put something around your mouth to stop you from crying out."

His words finally slipped into her foggy brain, and she clamped her mouth tight. "You won't have to," she said but started to shudder and shake as her body was overwhelmed with pain with his every step. "What happened?" she whispered.

"You've been shot," he said.

She laid in his arms, trying to absorb that information. But none of it made sense. "Why?"

"I don't know. I'm trying to keep us out of sight, but that's pretty damn hard too."

She was aware that they were running along the edge of the beach. "Can't they shoot downward on us?"

"There have been no other shots," he said. "Not since the initial one that took you down."

"Where'd they get the weapons?"

He didn't bother answering, and she realized she was

talking in order to take her mind off the searing heat in her shoulder. "I guess they missed, huh?"

He gave a broken laugh. "I don't know how you can say they missed," he said. "You've been shot."

"Yes, but I imagine they were trying to kill me and not just hurt me."

"Maybe," he said. "I'm not giving them a second chance. And it's not easy to shoot downward. It's easier to shoot down than up, yes, but I'm a moving target. That's doubling the difficulty."

"Is it bad?"

"No," he said. "You'll live."

But she realized that he was huffing as he carried her. Her need for answers and to talk was throwing him off his stride. "I'm sorry," she whispered.

He twisted to stare down at her. "For what?"

"For always being a problem," she said. He tucked her closer, almost as if trying to hug her, but that motion caused her shoulder to flare up in burning pain. She wished she could shut it off, but there was no way to do so. Every step pounded through her. She whispered, "I think I'll be sick."

"No," he said. "You're not allowed to be."

That startled a laugh out of her and settled her stomach somewhat. But then he had to take several different jolting steps as he moved down off the rocks, and, instead of feeling the bile crawl up her throat again, all she could see were black spots.

When she woke the second time, he was carrying her on a much more even surface. "Did I faint?" she whispered.

"You did," he said, his voice cheerful. "I'll bug you about that later."

She gave a half laugh. "And yet, you still carried me.

Why didn't you just dump me somewhere so I wouldn't be such a problem?"

"Well, that won't happen," he said. He stepped inside a building, and immediately she was awash in coolness.

"I'm glad we're inside," she said. "Only where are we?"

"The hospital," he said.

She groaned. "He won't want to see us."

"We have money. We can pay," Ryker said. "So that's not a problem. He'll look after you."

Even in her wonky mind, she could hear voices rushing toward them. She was laid on something cool and hard. Her body was readjusted and then her T-shirt was gently cut off her. She opened her eyes and looked up at Ryker, who hovered atop the two other people.

"That was my only shirt," she whispered.

"I'll get you a new one," he promised.

She let her eyes drift closed again until they started poking her shoulder. She cried out in pain and heard the muffled voices, but she was not quite far enough away to be unconscious. Finally, she understood that she was being rolled slightly and, with great difficulty, they flipped her and rolled her over a little bit so they could check the back of her shoulder. And then she heard, "It's gone clean through."

"Is that good or bad?" she asked.

"Well, good, except for the fact that you've got a shoulder blade with a hole in it now," he said.

She opened her eyes, and, for some reason, all she could think about was a hole literally in her shoulder, letting light through, and that image wouldn't leave her alone. Of course it was foolish, but the pain made her thinking completely cloudy. She laid back as she was injected with something. "I hope that's a painkiller," she murmured.

"It is," he said. "We have to go in and dig around to make sure the wound is clean, and this will help get you through it."

She stared up at him. "No surgery?"

He shook his head. "No, but this will probably be worse." And he gave her a heavier dose.

She closed her eyes and went out.

When she awoke for the third time, her eyes studied the ceiling above her, wondering where she was. She rolled her head to the side and cried out. Instantly, she recognized Ryker as he raced toward her.

"Don't try to move," he murmured.

"Why not?" she snapped.

"I see the drugs make you angry," he said with a note of laughter.

She glared up at him. "What happened?" she asked, reaching up and then crying out again.

He gently returned her arm to the position it was in. "I said, *Don't move.*"

She stared at him for a long moment, waiting for everything in her brain to tumble back into place, and she remembered being shot. "Did you catch him?"

"No," he said. "I've stayed here with you."

"You should have gone after him," she said childishly. "Otherwise, he'll shoot somebody else."

"Maybe," he said, "but it's hard to say. And you're my first priority. I wouldn't leave you to take another bullet."

"I'm in the hospital," she said. "He's not likely to get me here."

"He won't get you at all," Ryker said. "I'll make sure of that."

She wanted to say something mean about how she'd

been with him when she got shot, but she didn't want to upset him. What was wrong with her? She was both cranky and miserable at the same time. She shuffled restlessly in the bed. "The pain is really ugly," she whispered, trying to hold back the tears.

"You could use another shot of painkiller," he said. "Let me find somebody."

And he barely stepped out, and she found herself lying here in the small room and wondering at the ugly turn of events in her life. Who would ever want to shoot her? But then, who'd want to kidnap her either? It didn't make any sense. As she laid here, she heard voices and looked up to see the doctor coming toward her.

He had a smile on his face. "How do you feel?"

She raised an eyebrow at his excellent English. "Like I've been shot."

"Good," he said. "So, right on target then."

She groaned. "If that's a joke, it's a bad one."

"Not a joke," he said. He pulled back the bandage ever-so-slightly to check the wound and smiled. "It's looking pretty decent. I'll give you another shot but not quite as strong."

"Why not?" she asked, hating the petulant tone in her voice. But the last thing she wanted was to be in so much pain.

"So you're not unconscious," he said.

She accepted that without explanation, yet she wondered why she wasn't allowed to sleep. Sleep sounded damn-near perfect right now. As soon as he was done and had disappeared, she looked at Ryker. "Why can't I sleep?"

"Because we're leaving soon," he said.

She frowned. "I don't like the sound of that." And then

she thought about it and realized just how much pain would be involved in order to move at all. "You know how much it'll hurt, don't you?"

He nodded slowly. "Do you want to go home or not?"

She winced. "Is that my only choice? Stay here and sleep happily, or go home and feel all kinds of pain?"

"For the moment, it is. Yes."

She groaned and said, "Well, it's not much of a contest, is it? What about the others? Have you found them?"

"I talked to Miles, and he's rounding them up."

"I wonder where they were," she said. "I just wanted to go for a walk in the village."

"Well, you got a bit of a walk," he said quietly. "But no more. We can't take any more chances."

"But what about whoever shot me?" she asked. "It makes no sense."

"I know," he said. "I'd like to figure out exactly what's going on. Only we're running out of time."

"Well, I'll stay here and nap, so why don't you go off and figure it out," she murmured as the painkillers kicked in. "The doctor may not have expected me to sleep," she said, "but I think I'll nap anyway."

And she drifted off once again.

RYKER STOOD THERE, his fists clamped on his hips as he stared at her. She wasn't supposed to go off to sleep again, but he wasn't surprised that she had. The shock was as traumatic as the wound itself. Just then his phone rang. He pulled it out and answered Miles. "She's okay," he said. "She's dropped off to sleep again."

"Any idea who was up there?"

"Not really. But unfortunately, I have an ugly suspicion," he said.

"Care to share?"

He hesitated. "I hate to do so in case I'm wrong," he said. "Have you got the other two?"

"Yeah, bags are packed. We're all in one room right now," Miles whispered.

"Anybody see a sign of Pablo?" he asked Miles. "Apparently, he checked himself out."

"I'm not surprised he did," Miles said. "When you think about it, he's been the one to get into trouble over any of this, and, if the guerrillas realize he survived, he'll be in deeper trouble. Not to mention, he skipped out on his medical bill."

"I covered some of the doc's expenses. But what the guerrillas did to Pablo at the creek almost seemed like it was a spur-of-the-moment thing." He paused. "I can't make heads or tails of it. Maybe we'll know more before we leave."

"Maybe," he said. "But the bottom line is, we need to make sure we catch that ship out of here tonight."

"I'm with you there. I also don't want anything else to happen to her."

"I got it. So, do you want me to come down and stand watch?"

"Well, we still have a couple hours," he said, "so it's still a bit early. Did the guys eat?"

"No, they haven't. I need to grab something for everybody and make sure we have supplies on the boat. It'll be a long, cold night tonight."

"Make sure you get something warm for her, a blanket or a jacket or something so she's not chilled on the water.

And I'll ask the doctor for extra pain meds too."

"Okay, will do," Miles said. He hung up, and Ryker pocketed the phone, then turned to head to see if he could catch the doctor. He stayed in the hallway until the doctor went by and then asked for some medication for Manila overnight. Afterward, Ryker headed to the front desk and paid for a half-dozen pain pills. He figured, after six pain pills, maybe they would already be on the ship, and he could get her into the medical center there.

He also paid cash for her care. The hospital appeared to be more than grateful that he had enough money to cover her medical treatment. And he couldn't imagine how hard it would be for the doctors to treat anybody and get reimbursed for their expenses, let alone their wages. Local remedies, in most cases, would be enough. Only if they ran into difficulties, like right now, which would make it harder to do without traditional medicine.

Ryker stared out at the evening sky that came down gently, wondering if they would have any more issues between now and nightfall. What he really didn't want to do was leave this shooting hanging. He was afraid that a whole lot more was going on here than expected, so what he had to do was track down an answer. And quickly.

He pulled his phone out and sent Miles a text. **Can you guard her?**

On my way, Miles responded.

Ryker stepped outside to wait at the hospital door, where he could still see her room. Fifteen minutes later, Miles showed up. "The guys promised they'd stay inside the room," he said. "I warned them that it was either that or they would miss their ride out of here. They both appeared to be quite eager to go home, so I don't think that'll be a problem."

Ryker nodded. He took Miles to Manila's hospital bed and said, "Chances are she'll be asleep for the next hour anyway. And honestly, that's the best thing for her right now."

Miles looked at him and nodded. "Are you expecting her to get attacked here?"

Ryker frowned. "It's possible, but I hope not. I want to figure out what the bottom line is here."

"Good luck with that," Miles said.

"I want to check out where the shooter was," he said. "See what I can come up with."

"Go then."

With that, Ryker headed out to the front of the hospital, then picked up the pace and ran to the spot where she had been shot. As soon as he reached it, he realigned to account for where the angle of the shot had come from and for the flash he'd seen. Then he scrambled up to the higher part of the cliff edge, looking for where the shooter had potentially been. A few minutes later, he found the crushed grass where the shooter had stood. It had been a rifle shot, and, of course, it was possible that the guerrillas tried to take her out. But they had to have had a reason. It wasn't just a random shooting.

As he sat here, looking around and trying to figure it out, he heard a voice.

"It wasn't us, you know."

He froze.

"Don't turn around," the voice continued.

"Wasn't you what?"

"We didn't shoot her," the voice continued.

"And yet, you saw it all happen?"

"We did," the voice said.

"Are you part of the guerrillas?"

"Yes, but we didn't shoot her. We came in to talk to some friends and family, and we were already heading back to our camps."

"Is that common for you?"

"No, not necessarily. Most of us in the camps are family. But some of us have people in other places."

"And you didn't shoot her, and you're telling me this why?"

"Because usually, when anything bad happens, we're blamed," the voice said. "Just so you know, it wasn't us."

"But you know who it was though, correct?"

Silence.

He repeated, "Correct?"

When there was no answer, he turned to look, and the person had disappeared. Ryker thought about going after them because he certainly could. But, if they hadn't volunteered that information already, what were the chances that they would volunteer it now? But they brought up a good point. The fact of the matter was, whenever there was bad news around here, it would go to them. Everyone would blame the guerrillas.

Ryker called out, "I really could use the help." A weird stillness surrounded him. Still, he tried one last time. "At least a hint."

"Someone you didn't expect."

And that was it. The voice drifted from a long way away.

And Ryker knew that, even if he tried to catch up with him, there would be no catching up. *Someone he didn't expect?* That would be pretty damn open to interpretation. He hadn't expected anybody to shoot her. Not really. But the fact of the matter was, somebody had tried to take her out.

Whether they weren't a good shot and had messed up or whether they only intended to wound, he was not sure. And he couldn't imagine anybody else taking a chance like that without hoping for the best result. And so then, why not keep firing? Why not keep trying to kill them? Maybe the shooter had been disturbed or had seen someone approaching from his vantage point that they couldn't see? Or were they afraid that Ryker would come after them? Because that's why he was here now.

Nothing else could be gained from where he sat up on the top of the edge though, so he carefully made his way back to where they had left all their bags and then farther down the cliff. He removed the rope at the same time too, not wanting to leave anything here. And then realized that they should have taken the rope in the first place. It was also possible that one of the weapons had been taken from their bags while they had slept too. They had left everything up on the top of the cliff here, and, although they'd come back within a few hours to collect their things, it may not have been fast enough. And then again, in a place like this, it might not have been difficult to get a weapon like that.

Slowly he made his way back down to the town, and, when he stopped in at the hotel, he asked if the manager was available. But he wasn't around either. When he asked how to speak with him, he was pointed to his house, which was back along the cliff edge and farther back in the village. Ryker made his way up to the house, where he rapped on the door. The manager opened the door with a loaded rifle in his hand and frowned at him. "What?"

He looked at him in surprise. "Wow. Expecting trouble?"

"Already had some," he growled. "What do you want?"

Ryker considered the possibilities, then said, "I wondered if you happened to see anything."

"I don't know anything," he said. "You already turned those two men in. You're not turning me in too."

"I wasn't planning on turning you in," Ryker said mildly. "I was asking if you knew about the man who had been at the hospital."

"No, I don't know anything," he said, and he slammed the door in Ryker's face.

Wondering what was going on, Ryker slowly walked back toward the hospital. How was it that they didn't know anything? And, of course, he realized that they did know something. It's just that nobody was willing to talk.

He had two working theories. The manager with his loaded rifle seems to imply that maybe he had guerrilla problems of his own. So, he wasn't a guerrilla sympathizer? Or, hell, he could have been but now found himself on the receiving end of their *coaxing*? Granted, Ryker's best theory, in his opinion, was that Pablo had some sort of a way to make the manager and the hospital staff stay quiet or he'd paid them. Considering how poor people here were, Ryker suspected payment was part of it.

He slipped into the hospital and walked up to the receptionist. In a low voice, he asked her again if she had seen Pablo when he left.

She immediately shook her head.

"I know you did," he said. "And I know he paid you to stay quiet, and I don't know how he did that because he said he had no money."

She stared at him. Her eyes were wide but darting to the

side. He looked around, and another woman came toward him with a big a frown on her face. He leaned back and said, "I was looking for information on Pablo."

"We told you that he left this morning," she said briskly. "He checked himself out."

"And I left money to cover his treatment," Ryker said in a mild tone. "But that doesn't mean you don't know where he went."

"I don't know where he went," she snapped.

"Except," Ryker said, "that he felt he needed a safer place to go. So I'm sure somebody here may have offered him some shelter. Particularly for money."

She shrugged. "I don't know anything about it."

He wondered at that, but the woman turned and stalked away. He glanced at the receptionist and said, "Do you want to add to that?"

She bit her lip. He opened his wallet and brought out a one-hundred-dollar bill and dropped it in front of her. Her gaze widened, and she looked around, then quickly snatched up the money. "Two guerrillas came here, looking for Pablo. He got scared and paid her for a place to stay."

"And where did she let him stay?"

"Her husband's the manager at the hotel," she said. "She told him that he could stay there."

He thought about that and realized the man's attitude was more likely because he probably had Pablo sitting in the back of his house at the time of Ryker's visit—but the loaded rifle probably meant the two guerrillas had already been to his house earlier. He nodded and said, "Thank you." And he quickly disappeared out the front door of the hospital.

While he walked back up to the same house, he texted Miles.

Miles contacted Ryker by phone and asked, "Any reason for checking up on Pablo?"

"It's a confirmation on my nagging suspicion that he's not as safe as he thinks he is," Ryker said, back at the manager's house almost immediately, and, this time, when the man opened the door, the manager's face turned uglier and the rifle was still pointed at Ryker's face. "I understand that Pablo's here," Ryker said quietly.

"I don't know who you're talking about," the manager said.

"Well, I don't believe you," he said. "I would like to speak to Pablo."

"No," he said.

"And why is that?" Ryker studied the man's florid face. "Are you the one who's hurting him, or are you the one who's protecting him? Have the guerrillas already paid you a visit today?"

"I don't need to protect him," he said. "He was just looking for a place to sleep."

At that slip, Ryker nodded and said, "And why is that?"

"I don't know. Why do I care?"

"Maybe it's nothing," Ryker said. "So then why are you so upset that you offered a stranger a room for the night?"

The man's shoulders relented, and he nodded. "My boss doesn't like it."

"Why not?"

"It takes money from him," he said. "None of us are allowed to house anybody overnight. Otherwise, he gets really angry."

"And, of course, it's a small village, and everybody knows." *Well,* Ryker thought, *that was partially true.* He figured the manager was too scared to mention the guerrillas were here.

The manager nodded. "We all need money," he said.

"But Pablo has no money," Ryker said.

The man shrugged and said, "He can get some."

"How?"

"I don't know how, but he said he has money, and he'll bring it and pay us. Later today."

Personally, Ryker thought that was a load of shit. But, if these people were willing to do that on trust, then great. "What else does he want?"

"He's trying to get home," the man said.

"That makes sense, sort of," he said, *especially with two guerrillas on his tail.* "And is that something that can be done?"

"Eventually, yes. There are people traveling from village to village. He can get there, but it will take a couple weeks, and he needs money for that too."

"So he has lots of money then?"

He shrugged. "I think so."

"Good," he said, "but I still need to talk to him."

At that, the manager seemed much less hesitant. He stepped back a little bit and looked around, then said, "Pablo, Ryker wants to speak with you."

Instead, a scuffle was heard in the back of the house. The man frowned. "Pablo?"

Ryker bolted to the left and raced on to the back of the house in time to see Pablo moving quickly toward the woods. Ryker caught Pablo halfway and spun him around, only to have Pablo pull out a handgun.

Now, where had he gotten that? Then Ryker knew. Their own duffel bags most likely. He looked at it and, holding up his hands, asked, "Whoa. What's going on here?"

Pablo shook his head. "I want to go home."

"I get that," Ryker said. "I was looking for a way to get you home, but I don't understand what's going on."

"You don't have to understand," he said. "I need to go home."

"Why?"

He took a deep breath. "I have to."

"Why?" he insisted.

Pablo shrugged and said, "You won't understand."

"I do understand. The guerrillas are still after you." But then, as he studied Pablo, something else clicked in his brain. "Some people will do anything to move ahead in life. The other guide. Are you trying to get home before he does?"

Pablo looked at him in surprise and then shook his head slowly.

"No, of course not," Ryker said. "Because he can't go home, can he?"

Pablo frowned.

"That's where you got the money, right?"

At that, Pablo looked scared.

"You killed him. You took his money, and you're the one who cleaned out each of the three people on the American team. You took all their stuff too."

Pablo took several steps back.

"And now you want to get home fast enough so that you can't get caught here, not by the local authorities, not by the American team and not by those two guerrillas in town looking for you."

"I don't know what you're talking about," he said.

"I do," Ryker said slowly. "It's not that you weren't trying to be a guide, but you didn't intend on going home poor, did you? And you planned to take over your uncle's business. It wasn't your uncle trying to get rid of you. He was trying to give you a step up in life. Old Man Alejandro was your mentor. But instead, you went after him."

Pablo laughed and said, "You don't know anything." His tone was bitter. He pocketed his gun. "And I really don't have time for this." And he turned, but, instead of going back up the cliff, he headed down to the manager's house. Ryker thought about stopping him. Only, as he turned to follow, Pablo fired several shots in Ryker's direction. Warning shots nonetheless, but the meaning was clear. Following meant facing Pablo's wrath.

Ryker slowly walked back, trying to work out how all this was put into play, when Miles contacted him and said, "And what's going on?"

"I found Pablo. He's at one of the houses just behind the medical center up here, close to the cliff."

"Is he okay?"

"Well, he's moving well enough," Ryker admitted. "But I'm wondering if he isn't responsible for the older guide's death."

"What?" Miles asked.

"Yeah," he said, walking slowly toward the hospital. "I'll be down there with you in about ten minutes. I'm just working my way through this."

"But why would he do that?" Miles asked.

"I think it's so he could take over his uncle's business."

"But he said his uncle was trying to take *him* out."

"Yes, that's what he said. But I wonder how true it is. I wonder, if we dig into this a little further, would we find out his uncle and Old Man Alejandro *were* trying to help Pablo up in life, and, instead of wanting that assistance, Pablo wanted to be the big chief and take it over?"

"I don't think he liked being out in the jungle."

"Maybe not," Ryker said. "But this way, he could hire other guides, like his uncle did. And then he could stay home and not come back here."

Miles was silent for a moment. "That seems pretty far-fetched."

"Not when you add in two guerrillas have already been searching for him this morning, so Pablo stole one of our guns to protect himself. In fact, he just protected himself from me moments ago," Ryker said with a sigh. "It doesn't make complete sense yet to me. And it's not like we could ever prove it either. Anyway, the hospital is just in front of me. I'll be there in a few minutes."

He pocketed his phone and headed into the hospital, where Miles waited. They exchanged knowing glances but didn't say anything in front of Manila.

As Ryker approached, Manila was just waking up. She smiled up at him. "Hey."

"Hey yourself," he said, walking over and dropping down to kiss her lightly. "How are you feeling?"

"Pretty shitty," she said with a wan smile. "But I'll live."

He nodded. "Understood. Sorry about that."

She shook her head. "It is what it is. Did you find Pablo at all?"

He nodded and said, "But it's a little weird. He was acting pretty strange."

"He sure is," she said. "But then, it's also our life at the moment. I just want this whole episode over with."

Ryker looked at Miles and smiled. "Do you want to grab some food?"

"Sure," he said. "Stay here with her, and I'll buy food from the hotel to bring back."

"That'll be good," Ryker said.

And, with that, Miles quickly disappeared.

Ryker pulled up a chair. "I'm trying to figure out who shot you," he said. "And honestly, I'm not getting anywhere. I did talk to somebody. One of the guerrillas who had been in the village"—*to find Pablo*—"and was heading back when you got shot. I didn't get to see who it was, but he said they saw you getting shot, and it wasn't them."

"Wasn't them?" she asked in confusion.

"Yes, as in, it wasn't one of their fighters."

"But if it wasn't," she said, "who was it?"

"Well, the message I got said it was somebody who I didn't expect."

She stared up at him. "I'm so confused."

"I know. I am too."

"Well, if we can leave on time," she said, yawning, "none of it will matter anymore."

"I hear you," he said, as he squeezed her fingers. "I'll ask the receptionist to see if we can get some coffee."

"Sure," she said. "That would make me happy."

Ryker stepped out and talked to the nurse at the front, a different one this time. She nodded and said that she would bring some drinks for them. He then walked back to Manila's hospital room, thinking about everything that had gone on. He wondered if this really would stop here or if it would continue and be something much uglier. He frowned at that.

As he stepped into her room, he asked, "Is there any reason for Pablo to shoot you?"

She stared at him in shock. "No, of course not. Why would there be?"

He shrugged. "I don't know. Pablo was acting weird."

"Maybe," she said. "But he's not in his own village, and he wants to go home. I don't know how that'll happen, but maybe he has a way. Maybe somebody from his family will help him get back there."

"He could also cross the jungle again," Ryker said. "It might take him a couple days, but it's not an impossibility."

"But better if he doesn't go alone," she argued. "That can't be good."

"Maybe not," he said. Just then, the nurse arrived and brought a trolley with some coffee and water. He helped Manila to sit up and then brought a small table over for her. He thanked the nurse and brought Manila a cup of coffee and some water. She drank the water thirstily. And then realized he'd forgotten to get her a shirt. "I have a spare shirt in my pack," he said. "I'll head back to the hotel and get it for you."

"Do you think I still need a guard?"

He frowned at that. He looked over to see the nurse standing there, staring at the two of them in surprise.

"You don't need a guard here," she said. "Just a few of us in town are guerrilla sympathizers."

"I know," Manila said. "I'm just a little worried. I was shot, so I don't want the same shooter to come in and find me here."

The nurse looked at Ryker and said, "If you won't be very long, I can stay here with her."

Ryker considered it and pulled out his phone. "Hey, Miles. Have you left the hotel already?"

"Yeah. Why?"

"Grab a spare T-shirt of mine for Manila. They cut hers off when we entered the hospital."

"Well, if you want, I can come straight there, and then

you can run up and get the T-shirt," he said. "I'm a few blocks away. Let me come now."

Ryker thanked the nurse and said, "My partner will come to sit with her while I leave."

The nurse nodded and walked out.

He thanked her profusely because it really was an act of kindness. But then suddenly, Miles showed up with a big grin on his face. "Go, go, go, go. The guys are getting restless though."

Ryker nodded and raced from the hospital, then headed toward his room in the hotel. He didn't know what to do about the two guys still standing outside, guarding. He didn't even think of it as he headed into the other hotel room, but they watched him go in there and then frowned. He ignored them and closed the door to find both Benjamin and Andy sitting there.

"Why the hell can't we go out and do something?" Benjamin whined.

"Stop pissing me off. We'll be leaving soon, with or without you," he said. "Make sure you're ready and packed." He opened up his bag and searched through it to find his spare T-shirt. With that in hand, he closed to pack up. But then he stopped and noted that his bag full of weapons had been opened. He looked at it, frowned and asked, "Were either of you in this bag?"

They both shook their heads. "We haven't even been here very long," Andy said. "We didn't touch anything."

Ryker gave them each a long and measured look, then glanced back down, his mind immediately cataloging that a rifle was gone and so was a handgun. He knew that Pablo had the handgun. And, most likely, the missing rifle was the one that had been used against Manila. The tumblers in his brain were falling into place. He glared at Benjamin just to see him flinch.

Ryker thought more about it and then reached down and picked up both bags and walked out with them. He didn't give any explanation, and the two guys standing watch on the other room cried out and said, "Hey, what are you doing in that room?"

He glanced at them. "You guys suck as watchdogs."

"Why?" asked the younger of the two.

"Because Manila was shot. She's in the hospital." And, with that, he raced down the stairs.

One guy followed and said, "But we were standing outside the other door, watching all day."

He nodded and turned to look at him, then asked, "What about those other guys? Did you see them?"

"Yeah, one," he said. "We saw him a couple times today."

Figuring he meant Miles, he said, "The other one dressed like me?"

The guy shook his head. "No, not him. The shorter heavyset older guy."

"You saw him several times going to this room?"

"Close to your room." The guy looked confused. He pointed back up the room and said, "Going to your room. Or, at least, the other room." And then he stopped, obviously not very clear as to just what he meant.

Ryker thought about it and nodded. "So, he was in the room that I just came from, earlier today, on a separate occasion?"

"Yes, several times."

"Did you see him take anything?"

He shrugged and said, "Sometimes."

"A weapon?"

He shrugged again.

Ryker asked, "So, how many times did you actually leave this place versus standing watch?"

"When we had to go to the bathroom," he said. "And sometimes we had to get food."

"So, even with two of you, both of you had to go to the bathroom at the same time, and both of you had to leave together to get food? Right?" he said. "That figures. So, in other words, you don't know what you saw and didn't see him leave."

The guy nodded. "I was really surprised when I saw him the second time because I hadn't seen him leave the first time."

"Of course not," he said. "Thanks." And he headed out and back to the hospital. As soon as he got there, he handed her the T-shirt and then pulled Miles outside. "So, were you aware Benjamin's been in and out of our hotel room?"

Miles shrugged. "I'm not surprised. Andy maybe has been too. So have we."

Ryker told him what the one guard said.

"Are you thinking that Benjamin took the weapons? In which case, why would Pablo and Benjamin help each other?"

Frustrated and irritated, Ryker looked at Miles and said, "I don't have a clue. I just know this all has to have an explanation somehow."

"Well, it will," Miles said. "This is something we need to get to the bottom of before we leave."

"What I don't want to happen," Ryker said, his tone forceful and adamant, "is to take back with us something that'll reverberate even at home again."

"Meaning?" Miles frowned. "I should keep an eye on Benjamin?" Then, looking around at Manila, he smiled at her and asked Ryker, "Do you want me to head for food or …?" And he left his words hanging.

"Go get food," Ryker said, mostly for Manila's benefit, then dropped his voice to add, "but keep an eye out for Pablo and watch Benjamin's every move. Something's going on here that I don't like at all."

"Will do."

"Miles," Ryker called out. When Miles turned around, Ryker said, "Watch your back."

On that note, Miles lifted a hand and took off. Ryker turned and headed back to Manila's hospital room.

"SO WHAT'S GOING on?" she asked as Ryker entered. "Lots of smoke and mirrors," he said.

"You didn't find out who shot me?"

"Not yet." He shook his head but told her what he discovered.

"So, are you thinking it was Pablo?" She stared at him in horror. "After all we did?"

"I'm not saying that," he said. "We *can't* say that yet."

"I'd love to talk to him and to see for myself," she said. When Ryker remained quiet, she asked him, "You don't think Benjamin shot me, do you?"

"Do you?" he asked her.

"Of course not. He's all piss and vinegar and no action. No balls. That man is a crybaby, a whiner."

"He doesn't like you. He's made that abundantly clear."

"Just like he hates any woman with a degree who makes more money than he does." She waved her hand. "He's all bluff and bluster. A blowhard."

He noticed Manila had the T-shirt on. "How did you get that over your shoulder?"

She laughed. "It's big enough that I could pull it up my arm and then pull it over my head without having to do much. At least I'm much more capable of moving now," she said as she sat up slowly. She pushed the table away and hobbled off the bed.

"Whoa, where are you going?" he asked, stepping closer.

"To the bathroom," she said. And she walked out of her hospital room door and to the bathroom across the hall. He waited outside while she went in and used the facilities. There, Manila washed her hands and her face. She was feeling a lot better, but then she was still on decent drugs. She took a moment to twist her hair up and in a braid.

When she stepped back out again, Ryker met her.

"I just wanted to get all the blood off," she explained.

He nodded in understanding. "I got it," he said. And he helped her as they walked back to her room. When there was a commotion outside, he looked at her, frowned and stepped out the doorway.

"It's probably nothing," she said.

But instead, it was something. It was Pablo, running. He still had the handgun, but he wasn't pointing it at anybody, just had it ready, like someone was after him. Ryker watched him closely. As soon as he was inside Manila's hospital room, he closed the door. Then he looked at her and Ryker and said, "I didn't mean to."

"Didn't mean to what?" she asked, turning to look at him in surprise. "You look so much better," she whispered. "Obviously you're feeling much better too."

He nodded and motioned at her shoulder. "Are you okay?"

"I will be," she said. Then she motioned at the gun. "Why are you carrying a gun?"

He took a deep breath. "Because I want to go home."

She stared at him in confusion. "Could you explain that, please?"

"I think somebody will try to kill me," he cried out.

Ryker stepped forward. "And why is that?"

Pablo gave him a haunted look.

"What have you done?" Ryker asked, pressing him for an answer.

Pablo shook his head and said, "I can't say."

"You have to," Manila said in a quiet voice. "At times like this, the truth is really what we need to set us free."

"It won't set us free," he said. "It won't set us free at all."

"And why is that?"

"Because I've done something terrible," he said.

She sat here, waiting. And when Ryker went to force the issue, she held up a hand and said, "Let him speak, Ryker."

Pablo looked at her with tears in his eyes. "I owe my life to all of you," he said. "I wouldn't have made it out of that jungle without you."

"And?" Ryker asked in a hard voice.

Pablo stared at Manila and walked closer but immediately, Ryker stepped between the two of them.

"Unless you give me that gun, you can't take one step closer to Manila."

Pablo stared down at the gun. "I didn't even think I could use it," he said. And he pulled out another weapon from his pocket, which turned out to be a knife. "And this was Alejandro's."

Manila stared at it in surprise. "That's the knife that you and he were always arguing about?"

He nodded. "Yes."

Ryker held out his hand and asked, "May I see it?"

Pablo shrugged and handed over the knife, but he didn't hand over the gun.

Ryker took the knife and said, "I want the gun too."

Pablo stared at it and then finally gave it over.

Ryker immediately put it behind his back, stuffed into his waistband, and examined the knife. "This was Alejandro's, huh?"

"Yes," Pablo said.

"And did you have anything to do with his disappearance?"

"I told him that I had thrown his knife into the jungle, and I pointed in a direction where I had it. I was partially teasing, and partially I really wanted the knife too. So we were fighting and throwing, and then I just—I picked it up, and I threw it. My boss was really angry at me, and he headed toward the jungle." Pablo was visibly shaking as he spoke.

"And then what happened?" Manila asked gently.

"I don't know," he said. "There was a weird scream, and then I didn't hear anything."

"Well, didn't you go look?"

He gave her the longest look and said, "No, I didn't."

She sucked in her breath. "Alejandro might not have been dead, you know?"

"The jungle is not a very nice place," he said quietly. "That cry … That cry was Old Man Alejandro dying."

"And so you feel responsible?"

"Not only do I feel responsible but somebody in your team told me that I was responsible and that I could be killed for it."

"Why would they say that? And why would you feel that way?" Manila asked. "Yes, it wasn't very good of you. That's not how you treat anyone. And being greedy is hardly the way to go through life."

"I really wanted his knife," he said. "I guess maybe, in my heart of hearts, I wondered, if something bad would happen to Alejandro, then I could keep his knife."

"Did you do anything deliberately to kill him?" Ryker asked.

Pablo shook his head. "Honestly, I didn't. But I did make it sound like I had lost the knife out in the middle of nowhere. And I had seen the guerrillas …"

At that, instant silence filled in the room.

"Oh my," she said. "So you told him where you lost the knife, and he went there looking for it, and you knew the guerrillas would find him. But why would they have killed him and not you?"

He took a deep breath, and he said, "I told them."

"No, hang on a minute," she said. And then she stopped and said, "Oh, so they had captured you, and, in order to get away, you offered up your coworker, the old guide. Is that it?"

"And you guys," he said slowly, tears coming to his eyes. "But I didn't know what else to do."

"Because they had you as a captive too. And then, when they did come and catch us, your coworker, the old guide, was missing because you had already handed him off to them, where they then presumably killed him?"

"They killed him," he said. "I did ask. And they said that he wasn't coming back anymore."

"And so then, when they took us prisoner, you realized that they weren't looking at you with any favor because you had already killed off your coworker."

He nodded. "But I didn't know that that's how they would do it until they caught me by the river and sliced me up. And they told me that was for my betrayal and for my lack of loyalty. And I know I deserved it," he said. "I know that." Then, in a softer voice, he continued, "I didn't mean to get him killed. I just had a greedy moment, and I was thinking of how much my life sucked when I didn't have any money, and I didn't want to be doing what I was doing."

"You didn't want to be out in the jungle?"

He shook his head. "No, I never wanted to. I never had any intention of being a guide, but my father and my uncle insisted, and so I went with Old Man Alejandro, but I hated all of it. I just want to go home."

She nodded. "So then what happened?"

He shrugged. "You know what happened. You guys saved my life, my worthless life. Now I have to return and explain to my family what happened."

"Well, will you tell them the truth?" Manila asked Pablo. He hesitated, and she nodded. "Of course not," she said. "Because that isn't coming home with any sense of pride, is it? You don't want them to know the truth."

"Would you?" he asked. "It's one of my worst acts. I'm ashamed of my own behavior, and it cost Old Man Alejandro his life."

"But it got you the knife," Ryker said in a dry tone. His arms were crossed over his chest.

Manila studied Pablo and said, "Did you shoot me?"

He shook his head. "No, I didn't," he said. "But somebody asked me to. Somebody tried to pay me to. But we had a big fight, and I wouldn't do it."

"Because you're trying to go home," Manila continued. "In order to go home, you'll need money to get all the way around the country again because you're not going back through the jungle, are you?"

He shook his head. "No, I'm not. I'll get a ride and work my way around. There are vehicles that go back and forth, but I want to make sure I get all the way home again."

"So somebody asked you to shoot me. Presumably using one of the weapons that Ryker here had, and then, when you didn't do it, he got mad at you. Is that correct?"

He nodded. "But I escaped him and the two guerrillas that came this morning, and I paid somebody to hide in their house." He slid a sideways glance at Ryker. "That's where you found me."

Ryker nodded, but his face was dark. "I hear you," he said. "And that's why you ran. And that's why you had a gun on you. You knew that you could get caught by one or the other."

Pablo nodded. "I have money," he said. "But I also took all the money from your packs before the guerrillas came. And so I have your money too."

She stared at him in shock. "You're the one who swiped our wallets? We thought the guerrillas did."

"I knew that they were coming," he said. "And you guys were getting ready for dinner, so I went through the backpacks and found what I needed. And I've been carrying them with me."

"The guerrillas didn't strip you clean when they sliced you up?"

He shook his head. "They didn't search very well," he said. "I hid them inside my clothing."

"Well, that's smart, at least," she said. "Any chance I can get my cards back?"

He bent down and pulled up his pant leg and, inside his boot, were indeed her credit cards and Andy's. "Do you have Benjamin's too?"

He winced and shook his head. "I did. At first. But Benjamin already has his back again."

At that, she stopped, sagged on the bed and whispered,

"Is he the one who asked you to shoot me?"

He looked up at her with shame in his gaze, and he nodded. "But I never intended to. I just needed the money. I didn't do it." Pablo nodded again ever-so-slowly. "Then he paid me the money that I had already taken from him once and promised more."

"And you said yes. And you took Benjamin's money that he paid you to shoot me because you want to go home and to never have to return to that jungle again, right?" Manila asked Pablo.

He nodded, his expression full of shame and guilt.

"So Benjamin shot me then, since you wouldn't, didn't he?" Her voice was barely a whisper when she spoke. She groaned and said, "Wow, so all of this blaming the guerrillas and all the rest was a simple case of Benjamin trying to get rid of me."

"I wonder how much Benjamin had to do with this from the beginning," Ryker said quietly.

"I don't know," Manila said. "But what will we do now?"

He held up his phone and said, "I've recorded Pablo's statement right here. So, if nothing else, we'll have some evidence to take back with us."

"I can't even imagine this," she said. "I'm absolutely dumbfounded." She looked back at Pablo. "Is there anything else you need to tell me?"

He shook his head.

"Did your uncle back home or did the old guide with you in the jungle have anything to do with the guerrillas?"

"No," he said. "I don't think so."

"So the guerrillas just came upon you?"

He nodded. "After they spoke with Benjamin."

Manila and Ryker shared a wide-eyed look.

"And they needed what?" Manila asked.

Pablo sighed. "I'm the one who told them what you were doing and what you had as skills and that you guys all had money. But, while they were taking out the old man guide, I went through your possessions."

She looked at Ryker. "I don't even know what to say."

"No," Ryker said, "I'm sure you don't. I can't say I'm too surprised about Benjamin though."

Just then footsteps sounded, and Miles walked in. He took one look at Pablo and said, "Oh, this is interesting."

Miles handed over a bag of food to Manila, but she simply set it down on the little table and said, "I'm not even sure I can eat. Honestly, I'm feeling pretty sick to my stomach."

Miles looked at her in surprise and asked, "Why?"

She motioned to Pablo and said, "You need to tell Miles."

And, with great difficulty but with a clearer voice, Pablo repeated what he had just explained to Ryker and Manila.

Miles stared at Pablo in shock. "So you had Alejandro killed to get a frickin' knife? Then you stole from the team who you had brought into the jungle as one of their guides, and, when you realized that the guerrillas wouldn't keep you because you were so disloyal and had betrayed your own coworker, your mentor, we saved you, and now, down here, you found that one of Manila's team members wants you to kill her because the guerrillas failed to?" He took a deep breath. "So you took money from Benjamin to shoot Manila—but didn't?"

Pablo nodded. "It sounds pretty bad when you say it like that."

"It *is* pretty bad," he said. "I don't even know what to say to you. But I have bigger problems now. And I obviously have to deal with Benjamin."

"I'm coming with you," Ryker said.

"And I'm coming with you two," Manila said, her tone heavy. "This is really my problem."

"Then let me come too," Pablo said.

"I think you have to," Ryker said. "Because you're accusing Benjamin of hiring you to commit a murder, and that's a pretty major charge in our world."

With that, Manila, with Ryker's help, got her boots back on again, and they walked outside of the hospital, carrying the same food that Miles had just delivered. She was pretty tired by the time they got back to the hotel, not to mention sore. The two guards sat outside, but they hopped to their feet and said, "Hey, what's the point of standing guard if she's not even here?"

"I want to ask you once more if you saw Benjamin, the old heavyset guy you mentioned earlier, leave with a rifle in his hand."

"We told you that we didn't see him leave with anything."

"Right," Ryker said. "I just wanted to give you a chance to change your story now. After all, he paid you."

Both men flushed. They looked at each other, and then their shoulders sagged. "He did. We figured you had probably more guns in there, and we didn't want to cross him. He did have a rifle in his hand."

"Right," he said. They turned and opened the door, then stepped in. There, Benjamin and Andy sat at the table, playing some game with toothpicks. Manila looked at both of them. Andy came over and gave her a gentle hug. She smiled up at him and said, "I'm really glad to be going home."

"I am too," he said. "Are you sure you should be walking around? I can't believe you got shot."

"Yeah, that's terrible," Benjamin said.

"What you really mean," Manila said, "is that it's terrible that you missed and that I survived."

Benjamin stared at her in shock. "What are you talking about?"

For her answer, she placed her phone on Play and let them listen to Pablo's story.

Immediately Benjamin picked up her phone and hit Stop, then tried to delete it. "You can delete it all you want," she said, "but I already emailed a copy to myself and to Global Mining Industries and to my university."

He stared at her in shock. "You can't really believe that little weasel, can you?"

"But I do. I think you put that tracker in my bag too. So you could always tell the guerrillas where I was. However, I'm surprised you had the guts to make the original deal with the guerrillas to kill me in the first place. Except that you probably only did that in order to save your worthless life," she said. "And they took your cash, but you couldn't exactly ask them for a refund when Ryker and Miles here saved us before the guerrillas could kill me. I find that funny on two levels."

"I don't have a clue about what you're talking about," he said. "You can't possibly believe Pablo."

"What am I supposed to believe?" she murmured.

"It doesn't matter," he sneered, "but trust you to believe anything but the truth."

"Then tell me what the truth is," she said.

He glared at the four of them standing around him, while she walked over to the bed and laid down.

To Ryker, she said, "And now what?"

"Good question," he answered.

"That's all you're saying lately."

He nodded. "Sorry about that, but some of this stuff has to play out as it's meant to."

At that, Benjamin hopped to his feet and, this time, he held a handgun in his right hand, waving it around as he spoke. He glared at Manila and said, "You're the one who ruined everything."

Ryker carefully slid into place behind Benjamin.

"I haven't ruined anything," she said. "I'm lucky that I'm even alive right now, what with the guerrillas, the jungle, you and your rifle. Apparently, this bullet wound is from you," she snapped, tired and finished with the ugliness of life. "What the hell will you do with that handgun now? I guess if you're close enough, your shot may actually hit your intended target."

"I don't know," he said. "But I want to be free to leave."

"Where will you go?"

"I've traveled the world over, sweetheart," he said. "I have more experience out in places like this than you'll ever have."

"Good," she said. "You and Pablo can go. He wants to return home. Maybe the two of you can get there yourselves." She motioned at the hotel room door. "Go. You want freedom? Go."

He hesitated and backed up toward the door, then said, "You'll let me walk out of here?"

"Why do I care?" she asked. "You're not coming home with us."

He frowned. "It's not over, you know."

"Well, it is for you," she said. "You won't have a job at Global. Your good ol' boy buddy who pushed to have you on this expedition has been terminated, just so you know. I'm sure the local law enforcement here will be looking for you too, since you fired a shot in their fair village, potentially stirring up a war between the villagers and the guerrillas, so you might as well return to the jungle and make peace with whatever end you have coming."

He shook his head. "No way. The jungle? The guerrillas? You can't believe any of what Pablo said. I mean, did you hear him? He had his mentor killed."

"And you also paid the guerrillas to kill me, then paid Pablo to kill me when your plan A didn't pan out," she said.

"That's a joke. He was going to shoot you himself."

"What was his motive?" she asked.

Benjamin shrugged and said, "That guy doesn't need a motive."

By this time, Ryker stood between Benjamin and Manila on the left side of Benjamin, while Miles was at the right side of Benjamin, standing slightly behind him as he continued to wave his gun hand in Manila's direction.

Benjamin lifted his handgun and pointed it at her. "I'm not sure I give a shit about anything else anymore. You've already trashed my reputation, and we're not even back yet. I won't have any luck getting another job in my field. But, as long as you're not around, I'll die happy. So I might as well kill you now."

She slowly sat up. "Do you hate me that much?"

"Absolutely," he said. "The fact that you got my job over me is absolutely disgusting."

"It was never your job to begin with. And you would

never be lead on any of these trips either. That's it? That's all this is about?"

He nodded. "Yes, that's all it's about. It's my job. It shouldn't have been yours. I know I won't get it now, but I want to make sure you don't either." And he tried to pull the trigger, but instead, another gun rang out. It wasn't his. He looked at her in surprise and looked down at his hand, now bleeding profusely. He started to scream.

She looked over at Ryker, who had shot him in the hand, and said, "You could have just killed him."

He looked down at her and smiled. "Not going to happen. We'll take him back, and he'll stand trial. This coward needs to face the consequences of his actions."

"Good," she said. "As long as it doesn't involve me." She collapsed on the bed and said, "God, when can we leave this place? I really, really hate it here."

"In about twenty minutes," Ryker said. "I'm sure this quiet little village will be happy to see us leave."

"I'm not going with you anywhere," Benjamin said. "And you can't stop me."

And then, in a sudden move, he lunged down and picked up the handgun with his one good hand and turned it on himself. He looked at her and said, "I hate you, bitch," and, right before he pulled the trigger, Miles grabbed his gun hand, breaking his left wrist and probably a lot of the manifold bones in his hand and the gun went off, shooting Benjamin in the foot.

The man fainted at the sight.

A moment of stunned silence followed before Manila finally mustered the words, "Shit. We won't make that boat, will we?"

Ryker laughed and said, "Yeah, we probably will."

"And why is that?"

Miles held up his hand and said, "Because of this. I had it all on tape."

She groaned. "We'll have to take him back with us, won't we?"

They nodded. "We will take him back. But we'll ask the hospital for a body bag."

"He's not dead, is he?" Manila asked.

Ryker chuckled. "No, but he'll wish he was." He and Miles shared a knowing grin. "Both his hands are injured, so we'll put him in the body bag, with his head out, so he can breathe fresh air, instead of dealing with adult diapers."

Manila made a face. "What about local law enforcement?"

The two guys out in the hallway opened the door and said, "Everyone just wants you all to leave. You're a very bad influence here."

She sighed, nodded, and said, "I agree with you."

With that, everybody moved into action. Ryker had Manila's pain pills that she *might* share with Benjamin later. Otherwise, his medical condition was deemed not an emergency by the local doc, especially since the navy ship would have a medic on board. So the body bag was secured from the hospital, and the two men who had stood guard over her were paid to carry the still unconscious Benjamin to the beach in the dark. The Zodiac arrived on time. Benjamin was loaded quietly but not so gently into the bottom of the boat, and Andy and Manila were helped in to take their spots at the front. Miles and Ryker were at the back.

Andy sat beside her, and, in a soft voice as they pushed off from shore, he asked her, "Are you okay?"

She looked at him sadly. "I will be. It's a shitty way to

end a trip like this."

"It is," he said. "It never occurred to me that Benjamin would do something like that."

"He's from a different generation and held a lot of anger inside," she said.

"And you're still making excuses for him," Ryker said, coming up behind her. He wrapped his arms around her. "How are you holding up?"

She nodded and said, "I'm holding. I'm tired and worn out, but I'm okay."

"Good," he said, "because this may be the worst stage of your life, but it's now over."

She looked up at him and smiled. "Promise?"

He leaned down, kissed her gently and said, "Promise."

Andy looked at the two of them and said, "I didn't even see this happening."

"Life's what happens when you are looking elsewhere," Ryker said with a laugh.

Andy looked at Manila. "So, is this for real?"

She nodded. "I hope so. It's one good thing to come out of this trip."

"Sounds like it," Andy said. "Well, it works for me. Does that mean you're not doing too many trips in the future?"

"It'll be a long time before I do another one in Colombia for sure," she admitted. "But I don't dare let this stop me from traveling the world."

"Besides," Ryker said, "if I'm not on a job, I can come with you."

She beamed at that. "Oh, I'd like that," she said. "I'd have my very own protector."

"It sounds like you need it too," Miles said with a laugh.

She grinned and said, "Maybe not anymore. Only clear sailing for the rest of my life."

"Well, there'll be hiccups," Ryker said with a laugh. "But not something we can't handle." And he linked his fingers with hers and held her close. Manila thought about everything that she'd been through so far and realized he was right.

There was nothing that they both couldn't handle. *Together.*

EPILOGUE

MILES RADFORD POURED himself his first cup of coffee and stepped out onto his tiny balcony. He was renting a studio apartment with a lopsided built-in desk and a small kitchenette, just big enough for what he needed at the moment. It was also month-to-month as he figured out his life. He had a lot of good options, but nothing necessarily had the same adrenaline-pulsing lifestyle that he was used to. Nobody who ever became a Navy SEAL ever considered what came afterward.

The average participation in the program was eight to ten years. He'd already done fourteen and was well past the point of moving on, but he couldn't stomach imagining himself as one of the brass behind a desk. He wasn't *past* anything. He preferred something much more subtle and better suited for him.

He couldn't describe it in specific terms, but helping Ryker out had been part of it. Plus, rewarding to Miles. It had been taxing, sure, and dangerous. But reaching the end of it and also witnessing Ryker's hell of a new beginning with Manila was a better end. Miles hated to admit it, but he was almost looking for something like that himself. Same as a hell of a lot of other men too, apparently.

He'd heard of various lucky-in-love factions within the navy. Obviously, he knew Mason and his team. And also

Levi, who'd set up Legendary Security with his partner, Ice, that also had this incredible matchmaking system. Both men were leaders in their own right but would deny their matchmaker status until they were blue in the face, but something was magical about Mason's and Levi's teams. And now something was magical about the Mavericks team.

It wasn't their official name, but it had been coined and had stuck. They had a Mavericks chat window, aka the command central, and a growing number of members on the Mavericks team. But, so far, two men at a time were assigned to a mission, and then the others worked in the background. Somehow each understood they were being tested and trained for something bigger.

Miles sometimes wondered if he even wanted bigger stuff. He had told Beta, his Mavericks contact, that he would consider leading another job, if it came up. Having helped Ryker, Miles's turn was next to lead an op. If he wanted it. That was one of the things that he liked most about this. They were given a choice—unlike in the navy, where they had no choices.

It had always been *You're part of the team, so you'll do this for your country*, and he'd always been happy to do so, until he got to the point where he wasn't quite so happy all of a sudden. He realized it when waking up morning after morning became something he dreaded. He then wondered how much longer he could do this, and, at that point in time, he knew it was already past his time to leave the more rigid military setup.

Honestly, Beta's call had come at the right time. Miles had gone out to help Ryker and, so far, hadn't looked back. But now Miles had this edginess and this sense of waiting, this questioning as to whether he would take on any new offer made by the Mavericks. Of course, instinctively Miles would because he had never yet turned anybody down when they needed help. Especially if it was a serious breach of keeping the peace in this world. He hated the fact that the world was such a mess and that teams like the Mavericks were required. They were simple, subtle and got the job done though, and he loved that part. He just didn't know what kind of job he would be sent on.

So far, they've been everywhere from Thailand and China to Alaska. England too. Kerrick had taken that first job. And now that he thought about it, Miles wouldn't mind going back to England. It was his home country, after all. He hadn't lived there in a very long time.

When his first cup of coffee was done, he got up and poured another one to hear his phone buzz beside him. He took the phone and his coffee out on the balcony to answer Beta's text.

Are you ready? Beta asked.

Miles stared at it for a long heart-stopping moment. He'd just been thinking about this moment, and now here it was. And still, he knew without hesitation what his answer would be. **Yes. Where's the job?**

England.

He smiled at that. That's where he had wanted to go.

Good. What part?

London.

Okay. Traveling on my own?

Package is being delivered right now. Use the alias. Details are in the microdot.

Sunglasses?

Yes. Call us after you've read it.

Just then his doorbell rang. He hopped up and ran to the front door, then signed for the package from a delivery guy and walked back out onto his balcony. There, he quickly opened the package to see his alias was still Miles. Only his last name was now Richardson. *Miles Richardson.* A play on words? His real name was Miles Radford. But it was close enough that he wasn't likely to have a problem with it.

A piece of double-sided tape held a tiny dot to the inside of the envelope, and he found a pair of sunglasses inside too. He put on the glasses and fitted the microdot in the corner, where the screw belonged, and watched as the data flowed on the lenses.

He poured himself a third cup of coffee and sat down before slowly studying the material as it moved across the lenses. He hadn't even checked his flight details, and that was something he should probably have done first. But he was too absorbed in what was going on because this wasn't a normal case. This wasn't government assistance. This was Interpol and MI6. But not a terrorist cell activity.

It was a serial kidnapper.

This concludes Book 6 of The Mavericks: Ryker.
Read about Miles: The Mavericks, Book 7

The Mavericks: Miles (Book #7)

What happens when the very men—trained to make the hard decisions—come up against the rules and regulations that hold them back from doing what needs to be done? They either stay and work within the constraints given to them or they walk away. Only now, for a select few, they have another option:

The Mavericks. A covert black ops team that steps up and break all the rules ... but gets the job done.

Welcome to a new military romance series by *USA Today* best-selling author Dale Mayer. A series where you meet new friends and just might get to meet old ones too in this raw and compelling look at the men who keep us safe every day from the darkness where they operate—and live—in the shadows ... until someone special helps them step into the light.

When his call came, the mission was the opposite of what he expected ...

Returning to his hometown of London, UK, was a happy surprise, until he realized what—and who—was involved. Out of his comfort zone when dealing with women sold into sexual slavery or even "collected," regardless Miles was determined to dig in deep, when he realized he knew the latest kidnapped victim. A woman who'd touched him years earlier. To think she might be suffering at the hands of a deranged serial kidnapper or, worse, could be sold in some human trafficking ring ...

Vanessa, tied up and blindfolded, has no idea why she'd been kidnapped. She does her best to obey her captor, even as she plots her escape. Her hope is that she's been reported missing and that the cops are looking for her. … They are, but so is someone else …

Keeping Vanessa safe at his side, Miles is taxed to the limit to unravel and to capture a serial killer who's lain undetected for decades, disguised as a serial kidnapper …

Find book 7 here!
To find out more visit Dale Mayer's website.
https://geni.us/DMMilesUniversal

Author's Note

Thank you for reading Ryker: The Mavericks, Book 6! If you enjoyed the book, please take a moment and leave a short review.

Dear reader,

I love to hear from readers, and you can contact me at my website: www.dalemayer.com or at my Facebook author page. To be informed of new releases and special offers, sign up for my newsletter or follow me on BookBub. And if you are interested in joining Dale Mayer's Reader Group, here is the Facebook sign up page.
http://geni.us/DaleMayerFBGroup

Cheers,
Dale Mayer

About the Author

Dale Mayer is a *USA Today* best-selling author, best known for her SEALs military romances, her Psychic Visions series, and her Lovely Lethal Garden cozy series. Her contemporary romances are raw and full of passion and emotion (Broken But ... Mending, Hathaway House series). Her thrillers will keep you guessing (Kate Morgan, By Death series), and her romantic comedies will keep you giggling (*It's a Dog's Life*, a stand-alone novella; and the Broken Protocols series, starring Charming Marvin, the cat).

Dale honors the stories that come to her—and some of them are crazy, break all the rules and cross multiple genres!

To go with her fiction, she also writes nonfiction in many different fields, with books available on résumé writing, companion gardening, and the US mortgage system. All her books are available in print and ebook format.

Connect with Dale Mayer Online

Dale's Website – www.dalemayer.com

Twitter – @DaleMayer

Facebook Page – geni.us/DaleMayerFBFanPage

Facebook Group – geni.us/DaleMayerFBGroup

BookBub – geni.us/DaleMayerBookbub

Instagram – geni.us/DaleMayerInstagram

Goodreads – geni.us/DaleMayerGoodreads

Newsletter – geni.us/DaleNews

Also by Dale Mayer

Published Adult Books:

Hathaway House
Aaron, Book 1
Brock, Book 2
Cole, Book 3
Denton, Book 4
Elliot, Book 5
Finn, Book 6
Gregory, Book 7

The K9 Files
Ethan, Book 1
Pierce, Book 2
Zane, Book 3
Blaze, Book 4
Lucas, Book 5
Parker, Book 6
Carter, Book 7

Lovely Lethal Gardens
Arsenic in the Azaleas, Book 1
Bones in the Begonias, Book 2
Corpse in the Carnations, Book 3
Daggers in the Dahlias, Book 4
Evidence in the Echinacea, Book 5
Footprints in the Ferns, Book 6

Gun in the Gardenias, Book 7
Handcuffs in the Heather, Book 8

Psychic Vision Series
Tuesday's Child
Hide 'n Go Seek
Maddy's Floor
Garden of Sorrow
Knock Knock…
Rare Find
Eyes to the Soul
Now You See Her
Shattered
Into the Abyss
Seeds of Malice
Eye of the Falcon
Itsy-Bitsy Spider
Unmasked
Deep Beneath
From the Ashes
Psychic Visions Books 1–3
Psychic Visions Books 4–6
Psychic Visions Books 7–9

By Death Series
Touched by Death
Haunted by Death
Chilled by Death
By Death Books 1–3

Broken Protocols – Romantic Comedy Series
Cat's Meow
Cat's Pajamas

Cat's Cradle
Cat's Claus
Broken Protocols 1-4

Broken and... Mending
Skin
Scars
Scales (of Justice)
Broken but... Mending 1-3

Glory
Genesis
Tori
Celeste
Glory Trilogy

Biker Blues
Morgan: Biker Blues, Volume 1
Cash: Biker Blues, Volume 2

SEALs of Honor
Mason: SEALs of Honor, Book 1
Hawk: SEALs of Honor, Book 2
Dane: SEALs of Honor, Book 3
Swede: SEALs of Honor, Book 4
Shadow: SEALs of Honor, Book 5
Cooper: SEALs of Honor, Book 6
Markus: SEALs of Honor, Book 7
Evan: SEALs of Honor, Book 8
Mason's Wish: SEALs of Honor, Book 9
Chase: SEALs of Honor, Book 10
Brett: SEALs of Honor, Book 11
Devlin: SEALs of Honor, Book 12

Easton: SEALs of Honor, Book 13

Ryder: SEALs of Honor, Book 14

Macklin: SEALs of Honor, Book 15

Corey: SEALs of Honor, Book 16

Warrick: SEALs of Honor, Book 17

Tanner: SEALs of Honor, Book 18

Jackson: SEALs of Honor, Book 19

Kanen: SEALs of Honor, Book 20

Nelson: SEALs of Honor, Book 21

Taylor: SEALs of Honor, Book 22

SEALs of Honor, Books 1–3

SEALs of Honor, Books 4–6

SEALs of Honor, Books 7–10

SEALs of Honor, Books 11–13

SEALs of Honor, Books 14–16

SEALs of Honor, Books 17–19

Heroes for Hire

Levi's Legend: Heroes for Hire, Book 1

Stone's Surrender: Heroes for Hire, Book 2

Merk's Mistake: Heroes for Hire, Book 3

Rhodes's Reward: Heroes for Hire, Book 4

Flynn's Firecracker: Heroes for Hire, Book 5

Logan's Light: Heroes for Hire, Book 6

Harrison's Heart: Heroes for Hire, Book 7

Saul's Sweetheart: Heroes for Hire, Book 8

Dakota's Delight: Heroes for Hire, Book 9

Michael's Mercy (Part of Sleeper SEAL Series)

Tyson's Treasure: Heroes for Hire, Book 10

Jace's Jewel: Heroes for Hire, Book 11

Rory's Rose: Heroes for Hire, Book 12

Brandon's Bliss: Heroes for Hire, Book 13

Liam's Lily: Heroes for Hire, Book 14
North's Nikki: Heroes for Hire, Book 15
Anders's Angel: Heroes for Hire, Book 16
Reyes's Raina: Heroes for Hire, Book 17
Dezi's Diamond: Heroes for Hire, Book 18
Vince's Vixen: Heroes for Hire, Book 19
Ice's Icing: Heroes for Hire, Book 20
Heroes for Hire, Books 1–3
Heroes for Hire, Books 4–6
Heroes for Hire, Books 7–9
Heroes for Hire, Books 10–12
Heroes for Hire, Books 13–15

SEALs of Steel
Badger: SEALs of Steel, Book 1
Erick: SEALs of Steel, Book 2
Cade: SEALs of Steel, Book 3
Talon: SEALs of Steel, Book 4
Laszlo: SEALs of Steel, Book 5
Geir: SEALs of Steel, Book 6
Jager: SEALs of Steel, Book 7
The Final Reveal: SEALs of Steel, Book 8
SEALs of Steel, Books 1–4
SEALs of Steel, Books 5–8
SEALs of Steel, Books 1–8

The Mavericks
Kerrick, Book 1
Griffin, Book 2
Jax, Book 3
Beau, Book 4
Asher, Book 5
Ryker, Book 6

Miles, Book 7
Nico, Book 8
Keane, Book 9
Lennox, Book 10
Gavin, Book 11
Shane, Book 12

Collections
Dare to Be You…
Dare to Love…
Dare to be Strong…
RomanceX3

Standalone Novellas
It's a Dog's Life
Riana's Revenge
Second Chances

Published Young Adult Books:

Family Blood Ties Series
Vampire in Denial
Vampire in Distress
Vampire in Design
Vampire in Deceit
Vampire in Defiance
Vampire in Conflict
Vampire in Chaos
Vampire in Crisis
Vampire in Control
Vampire in Charge
Family Blood Ties Set 1–3
Family Blood Ties Set 1–5

Family Blood Ties Set 4–6
Family Blood Ties Set 7–9
Sian's Solution, A Family Blood Ties Series Prequel
    Novelette

Design series
Dangerous Designs
Deadly Designs
Darkest Designs
Design Series Trilogy

Standalone
In Cassie's Corner
Gem Stone (a Gemma Stone Mystery)
Time Thieves

Published Non-Fiction Books:

Career Essentials
Career Essentials: The Résumé
Career Essentials: The Cover Letter
Career Essentials: The Interview
Career Essentials: 3 in 1

www.ingramcontent.com/pod-product-compliance
Lightning Source LLC
Chambersburg PA
CBHW071522110726
47908CB00003B/920